*The Kiss*

# *The Kiss*

# JOAN LINGARD

First published in Great Britain in 2002 by
Allison & Busby Limited
Bon Marche Centre
241-251 Ferndale Road
Brixton, London SW9 8BJ
*http://www.allisonandbusby.com*

A catalogue record for this book is available from the British Library

ISBN 0 7490 0557 2

Printed and bound in Wales by
Creative Print & Design, Ebbw Vale

JOAN LINGARD is the acclaimed author of over 40 books for both children and adults. She was born in Edinburgh and brought up in Belfast, the inspiration for many of her novels, including the compelling *Across the Barricades*. She was awared the MBE in 1998 for Services to Children's Literature. *The Kiss* is the result of a long-standing personal fascination with the painter Gwen John.

*For Francine*

# *Prologue*

It is raining, on a November afternoon, and cold. The woman standing in the shadows of the laundry doorway feels the chill of the pavement creeping up into her feet and ankles. From time to time she moves them, just a little, but otherwise she remains still, her bony hands clasped in front of her. Her eyes stay fixed on the large doors opposite. Her gaze is steady, except when a vehicle passes between them, and then it flickers. Occasionally a small cough grazes her throat.

The afternoon wears on, the light fades early, and the gas lamps splutter into life, making her draw further back into her refuge. Now the puddles on the pavement shine. She can hear faint music coming from the building across the street. Someone is playing the piano. It will be warm in that high-vaulted room, with the stove billowing forth heat to the assembled company; *he* will be there surrounded by women fawning on him, hoping for his favours. Once she, too, was made welcome at these Saturday afternoon receptions, but then she annoyed him and she could not bear the attention he gave to the other women. The attention he gave in particular to *her* of the glaring hair and the terrible hats calling herself his inner voice. As if he had need of any voice but his own! She looks like a painted weasel, this American, who has ordered all his other models from the studio. His friends detest her. But he appears to be bewitched.

A man stops. His shadow falls across hers and she can smell his breath, heavy with cigar smoke. '*Mademoiselle?*' She shakes her head and he hesitates for only a moment before moving on. She is often bothered by rodeûrs, men who follow her, who sit at cafe tables beside her; and she cannot understand why. She does not believe she is flirtatious. Her affections are already engaged.

Across the road, the wide doors suddenly burst open, spilling out yellow light and men and women with flushed faces and ringing voices calling out farewells. Faces turn up to the sky. Umbrellas are unfurled. The women embrace their host; the men wait and idly chat. Two carriages turn into the street and pull up, and when they have moved on there remains only one person on the pavement opposite. Even in this poor light one can see that he has a presence, this broad, well-built man, with the powerful head and full beard streaked with white. He may no longer be young but he emits energy. She can feel his energy in her hands when she holds them out. They tremble as if shot through with a lightning current.

Hesitantly, she moves out of the shadow. Alerted, like an animal sensing another presence, he turns his head. She steps over the flowing gutter and crosses the road. She hears him sigh.

'You'll get your death, standing in the cold and wet like that. How many times do I have to tell you?'

She is encouraged. He is not angry; she may walk

12

with him. He unfurls his umbrella and she falls in beside him. Before they reach the corner she manages to slide her hand into the crook of his arm. She loves the smell of his bulky coat and the warmth of it against her fingers. It is a fair step to the station, and of that she is glad, and would willingly walk with him all the way to Meudon, if that were possible. This is her time. She will have him to herself; the red-haired witch cannot claim him now, nor any of his other admirers or former lovers. She is glad, too, of the rain, for it is like a curtain cocooning them from the rest of the world. She finds its gentle patter on the dark arch covering their heads soothing to her nerves. They skirt the edge of the Place de la Resistance and arriving at the Avenue Bosquet turn north into it.

He continues to scold her a little. 'Are you eating enough? You're looking thinner again. You must eat. You can't paint if you don't eat.'

She is trying, she responds, though often she forgets.

'Are you still reading?' He wants to know; his interest is more than passing. She is able to please him there, telling him that she reads every day. He is a keen reader himself though it is a wonder to her that he can find time in his overflowing life. He likes to read the English authors Fielding and Richardson, and is deeply interested in classical Greece. He has been encouraging her to read Greek poetry and drama. Sometimes she retells stories from mythology to him that she hopes might give him ideas for his sculpture. She speaks now of Euripides.

'Like you,' she says, 'he believes that everything has beauty.'

Too soon, they are in the Boulevard de Montparnasse

and the station looms ahead. She longs to go home on the train with him, to prepare his evening meal, to sleep with him, to wake with him and rise to warm his morning milk. But there is another woman waiting there for him, his Rose, a peasant woman who has been with him for forty years and has borne him a son. She stays out there, beyond the confines of the city, awaiting his return each evening, stirring her cooking pots.

They enter the gloom of the station. Smoke hangs in the air; on the ground, travellers hurry to their platforms. He must leave her.

'Will you come to visit me soon?' She holds her breath. She has hardly dared to ask.

'I can make no promises,' he says.

She stays in most mornings sweeping and cleaning her room, going from time to time to the window to look down on the street. Sometimes he does come but she knows not to press him or to rail against the American duchess who distracts him and keeps him from his work. If she does she will only make him angry and her time with him will have been spoiled. She has made a fuss in the past about the woman and after one occasion he told her not to come to his studio again. Now she waits outside and he does not chase her away.

'Remember to look after yourself,' he tells her and with a glancing kiss on either cheek he has gone, into the moving mass.

She waits till his train steams out of the station, even though she knows that he will not pull down the window and lean out to wave. In the early days, not so long ago, only a few months, when they were first lovers, he would sometimes come to the window and then she could go home with a smile inside her. Her eyes ache with staring but the train is no longer there; its red rear light has dwindled into nothingness. She turns and makes her way back out of the station, stumbling a little, head bowed, bumping into hastening passengers, having to apologise. *Pardon, pardon* ...

She returns to her quiet grey room in the Hôtel Mont Blanc on the nearby Boulevard Edgar Quinet. She is shivering. She peels off her damp coat, walks out of her shoes. She goes to the table by the window and lights the lamp. Her notepaper is waiting there, the pen is lying where she left it earlier. She lifts it, plunges the nib deep into the ink-well and begins to write.

*'Mon Maître ...'*

# Chapter One

'Is that it?' he asks.

'Seems to be,' she says.

Together, they take a last look at the bare hall, at the grimy-edged spaces where the pictures used to hang; they glance up the uncarpeted stairs, hear the eerie silence. She moves first, turning her back. He tugs the door shut behind them. The damned thing has always been inclined to stick. They've been meaning to do something about it, for months. Years.

She holds up the keys. 'Will you take them or shall I?'

He shrugs. 'Doesn't matter. I could put them through the solicitor's letter box, if you like.'

'You won't forget? You know what you're -'

'For Christ's sake!'

The air between them has become charged, in that split second, has swollen up like a balloon. Then her shoulders slacken.

'Sorry.' She tosses the two sets of keys, he catches them against his chest.

He follows her down the path. The street is quiet. Few, if any, will witness their departure. Between drawn curtains the excesses of Old Year's Night are being slept off.

He goes round to the driver's side of the self-drive rental van, she makes for the family saloon parked behind it. It is stuffed full with bedding, downies and pillows, still slightly dented, showing where heads have rested, dragged from beds only this morning.

'See you there,' he says.

She nods.

In the back of the truck the two children sprawl amid brown grocery cartons. The girl is no longer a child, really, and would resent being called one; she has passed her fifteenth birthday. The boy is seven years her junior.

'Last run,' says their father breezily.

He edges the high-sided vehicle out from the kerb, away from the tall, terraced house. Desirable family residence, two reception, four beds, two baths, large kitchen, scullery, laundry room, large attic which may be used for storage or a studio. Garden front and rear. Mature trees. Good neighbourhood. Convenient for schools. Their ad said it all.

The girl, positioned by the window, lifts her head. The boy does not. He continues to gaze at his bunched up knees.

There is almost no traffic. The city seems unnervingly quiet.

'Fantastic day,' says the father. The sun is shining out of an ice-blue sky after days of hectic rain and wind. 'Good day for a walk on the Pentlands.'

There is no response form the back.

The trip takes only five minutes, as the driver is keen to point out. No distance at all. It isn't as though they're moving miles away.

'That's scarcely the point,' says the girl, silencing her father.

They are heading for a small enclave of Victorian

artisans' houses known as the Colonies which lie alongside the Water of Leith. He rounds the clock at Canonmills, then swings across into Glenogle Road.

'You know the Colonies were built by the Co-op in the second half of the nineteenth century? Workers who had never expected to own their own houses were suddenly able to do it on a mortgage-type basis.'

'You've already told us,' says the girl. 'What's so marvellous, anyway, about owning your own house?'

Her father concentrates on the road. Flipping on his indicator, he turns sharply right into one of the short, narrow streets. The road is little more than two car-widths wide, which means that he has to mount the pavement to ease the wide van past the line of parked cars on the left-hand side.

The houses here are terraced, too, but on a different scale; they were built in cottage-style architecture, consisting of an upper and a lower flat, the upper being reached by an outside stone stair. The stair is a distinctive feature of the Colonies, he is about to remark, then closes his mouth.

He pulls up. 'Well, here we are!'

The girl wrenches open the back door and vaults out, as light as a young roe deer. The boy stays in the van. The following car has stopped behind them.

'Four of the boxes are yours, I think,' says the father, heaving them out. 'Want a hand up the steps?'

'We can manage,' says the mother. She ducks her head inside the van and kisses the boy. 'See you soon, Davy love. OK?'

He nods.

The father kisses the girl. 'We'll just be along the road, Sophie, old pal.'

'It's all right,' she says. 'I don't *mind*. Really I don't.'

He waits until they have climbed the steps to their upper flat, then he jumps back into the driver's seat and begins to back up, which takes all his attention, with so many cars parked, and space being so tight. The streets are cul-de-sacs, running into the river.

Their upper flat - his and Davy's - is but two streets away and virtually identical to the other one.

'Well, son,' he says as he parks, having managed to squeeze into a space, just, 'this is it!' He hears his voice coming over as far too hearty. 'Our new abode.' Their flat is close to the river end.

At the top of the stair, he pauses to look over at the Water of Leith, Edinburgh's waterway. He can smell it, a damp, muddy smell. 'We might go fishing.'

'The water's yucky,' says Davy.

His father opens the door. The flat has a rather mouldy smell, well, of course it would, wouldn't it, as he says to his son, since nobody has been living in it for some time and in winter it doesn't take long for buildings to cool down and the damp to seep in. He is talking too much and his son too little. He wonders if he has talked too much all his life. If he had kept his mouth shut more when conducting his art classes he might not have ended up in this mess. He wishes he could go to the pub.

There are two rooms on the main floor, a sitting room at the front and a dining/kitchen to the rear. The lavatory is under the stairs in what once would have been a cupboard. The ceiling slopes perilously low over the bowl; he will have to mind his head when he gets up. There is no wash-hand basin, no room for one.

'We'll just have to wash our hands in the kitchen or nip up the stairs,' he says jocularly. There is a wash-hand basin and a bath up there, but no lavatory.

They go up the narrow stairs. One bedroom has a dormer window, the other a skylight. Both rooms are small. All the rooms in the flat are small. He wants to kick out the walls but he tells himself that the place will be easily heated which means they can save on fuel bills. One must look on the bright side! The jingle runs through his head, annoying him. He intends to take the dormer window for himself, having reasoned, to himself, that kids don't notice whether there is a view or not. He'd go nuts if he couldn't see out.

Davy throws his bag on the bed in the skylight room. The glass is grubby; the sky cannot be seen. They'll clean it, says his father, once he buys some Windowlene, and then Davy will be able to lie in bed and look at the stars. '"When midnight's all a glimmer,"' he quotes. 'Famous Irish poet wrote that.'

Davy shrugs, though his father knows that he likes poetry, but today he is not going to like anything and who could blame him? His father swallows. He sure as heck could use a drink. They didn't drink much last night, he and Rachel, in spite of it being Hogmanay. They were busy and not in the mood, and old friends stayed away, trying to be tactful, or else just embarrassed. Not that they were doing anything unusual, in this day and age, except in the eyes of a few elderly people like his mother. Ah, yes, his mother. He puts the thought of her out of his mind. He has enough to cope with at the moment.

'Where will you do your work, Dad?' asks Davy. 'There's no place for a studio here.'

'We'll have to see,' says his father. He hasn't done any-thing, anyway, for a long time, forever, so it seems, not since the day he was called into the head's office.

'Sit down, Cormac,' said Archie, without lifting his head. He was fussing about with some papers on his desk, which Cormac could see he was not looking at. They were friends, he and Archie; they'd known each other since their student days, had shared a flat for a while. They often had a pint in the pub together after school and they went to international rugby matches togeth-er, enjoying pleasant rivalry when Scotland played Ireland. They ate in each other's houses. Nothing fancy, no fuss. Kitchen supper, kedgeree, fish pie, that kind of thing. There was no formality between them or their wives. There was no formality between Archie and any of his staff. He was a casual, pullover-wearing, no-stand-ing-on ceremony head. Popular with both staff and pupils, which took some doing. He had been popular as a student, too. His prowess on the rugby field had contributed to that; he'd played for the university's first fifteen and represented Scotland in its under twenty-one team. He helped coach the school team and could outrun most of them still. Cormac had never been much of a rugby player himself, had played at school when he couldn't avoid it but had preferred football which he found less brutal. As for other sports, pool was the only game he occasionally indulged in, where-as Archie played a good game of golf and tennis and was a competent skier. On the surface, then, it did not seem as if he and Archie would have much in com-mon. At university, Archie was studying mathematics; he was doing sculpture. But from the first moment the two men met they hit it off; they seemed to complement each other and there was no element of competition between them since their sights professionally were set on different things. Cormac found Archie's easy, open manner and self-confidence engaging. He may not be very deep, he had said once to Rachel, but he's sound. And how reassuring it was to be in the company of someone who was sound, who wasted no time in self-doubt and looking back.

Cormac did not feel happy in Archie's company now. He edged his chair a little closer to the desk.

'What's up, Archie?' he asked.

Archie sighed again. 'This isn't going to be easy for me, Cormac.' He was twiddling a pen between his thumb and forefinger. He dropped it and had to look Cormac in the eye. 'We've had a complaint made against you, I'm afraid.'

'Oh no.' Cormac groaned. 'Not Clarinda Bain's mother!'

So you know what it's about then?' Archie looked taken aback as if he had expected Cormac to plead total ignorance.

'I suppose I can guess. Clarinda's been behaving like an ass so I called on her mother who went on to make wild accusations about the visit to Paris.'

'They were fairly wild.' Archie sounded glum.

'A load of old cobblers. You didn't believe her, did you?'

'It's not up to me to believe or disbelieve, Cormac, not at this juncture. That'll be be for other people to decide. I'm not even allowed to discuss it with you. But why didn't you come and talk to me about it before?'

'I did try to, the day after we came back from France, in the pub, after school.'

'You mentioned Clarinda's name, I remember that. You said what a keen pupil she was and eager to see everything in Paris, but you didn't make it *clear*, at least I didn't pick up that there were well, *sexual*, implications.'

'Maybe I didn't,' said Cormac. He'd thought Archie had almost been trying to ward off his confidence, as if he'd heard rumours and didn't want or didn't need them to be spelled out. Or maybe he'd thought he'd been going to hear an admission of guilt? It had been an awkward meeting and Cormac had been aware of his own reluctance to spell everything out. Then Ken Mason, another member of staff, had came in and joined them, and so the subject had changed.

'You should have come back to me on it,' said Archie.

'I suppose I thought it would blow over. You know how it is when you don't quite want to face up to something?'

'Yes.' Archie nodded. 'Yes, I do know. Sometimes life takes odd directions, doesn't it, when you least expect it?'

Cormac had never known Archie take an odd turning, or act out-of-character. His very stability was like a rock for school life to revolve around, and he was a sympathetic listener.

'It wouldn't have made any difference even if you had talked to me. I'm bound by a set of rules, Cormac, you know that. I have no option but to suspend you, as from now. On full pay of course.'

'This very minute?'

'I'm afraid so. There'll be an inquiry. It has to go through the proper channels. Oh, and by the way, you're still under contract to the Education Authority so you are obliged to stay put, to be available if called upon.'

'So there's to be no skiving off to South America?' His attempt to make a joke stuck at the back of his throat.

'I am sorry, Cormac. Deeply sorry.'

Cormac nodded.

'And I won't be able to see you socially, either, you realise that, don't you, until this business is sorted out?'

Cormac sat for a moment, then he stood up, and putting one foot before the other moved as if in a dream from the quiet of the headmaster's room into the corridor which was alive with the surge of young, vigorous bodies heading for the freedom of the open air. It was the start of morning break. He banged into some of the bodies, did not even hear their yowls of protest. 'Watch where you're going, Mr Aherne!' He should have done that years ago. That's what his mother would have said to him, had she been there.

It was break-time, for which he was grateful. His art room was empty. Someone had tipped a chair on its side in their hurry to get out. Automatically, he picked it up and set it to rights. He'd been teaching a first year-class when he'd been summoned, trying to enthuse them about Art. Commitment, he had been telling them, that was the key; no artist had ever achieved anything without commitment. And passion. The ultimate stage was obsession. You had to be obsessed, seized by the throat. They had listened to him, mesmerised, or so it had seemed, though perhaps they had just been puzzled. Some of them were obsessed by football, weren't they? That had got them, the boys who'd been shuffling their feet; that had helped to focus them. They were beginning to see a glimmer of light when the door had opened to admit Miss Dunlop, the school secretary, with her spectacles dangling from a chain around her neck, come to summon him. 'Mr Aherne, Mr Gibson would like a word.'

Ah, the power of a word. It could change a life.

He would be summoned again, to make his case, perhaps even at the High Court, where he would be compelled to listen to a flow of words, of evidence against him, if, after investigation, it was thought that he had a case to answer. Did he?

He gathered up his papers, shoved books into a carrier bag, unpinned his Rodin posters and photographs from the wall, and left the building where he had been employed, some would say gainfully, for the past fifteen years.

'I'm going to phone Grandma,' Cormac shouts up the stairs to Davy, who is moving around in his new room. Stay out of the way, is what he means. 'Grandma Aherne,' he adds in a mutter and closes the living room door.

He has decided he'd better do it in case she should ring their old house to wish them a happy New Year. So, all right, maybe she has never done it before but she could decide to do it now, couldn't she, for the very first time, and if she got the dialling tone going on and on and on without the answering machine chipping in she might begin to wonder? To panic, even. So he has been telling himself. He flexes his fingers and punches out the number.

She answers at once as if the phone has been at her elbow.

'I thought it might be you,' she says and waits.

'Happy New Year, Ma.'

'Let's hope it will be a better one than last year.'

'He clears his throat and quickly tells her his news.

'This isn't your idea of a joke, is it, Cormac?'

He tells her it is not. Would that be his idea of a joke, for goodness sake?

'I never know with you, Cormac. You're like your da when it comes to joking. You've a queer sense of humour at times.' She sighs and gathers her breath and he keeps his head bowed and the receiver well away from his ear while the storm flashes and the breakers roll relentlessly over him, making, as they crash, a deafening roar. When they have subsided, he hears her say. 'I always thought it was a mistake for you to marry a Protestant.'

'For Christ's sake, Ma, it's time to give up all that old rubbish!'

'Rubbish! Is that how you refer to your faith?'

'I haven't been a practising Catholic since I was eighteen, and well you know it.'

'That's part of your problem, Cormac. Faithless.'

She might well be right, he is not prepared to dispute that. He is conscious of the vacuum inside him which once he could fill with Hail Marys and pleas to God to have mercy on his soul. He still believes he has a soul for inside him somewhere there is something that he can give no other name to and there are times when he has longed to sit in front of a flickering candle and close his eyes. And find peace. That, of course, is the attraction, the notion that seduces. He has done it a couple of times, crept up the steep, exposed steps to St Mary's Cathedral and lit a candle. And sat there with an empty mind, feeling like a hypocrite, glancing idly round in case his mother or one of his holy aunts might be sitting at the back watching him. Spying on him. There wasn't much chance of that since the Irish Sea yawned between them, he could thank God for that, at least. But he felt their eyes, nevertheless.

'Are you still there, Cormac?' His mother is making the line click at the other end.

'Yes, I'm still here.'

'Of course you had to marry her, didn't you?'

'I did nothing of the sort. We knew Sophie was on the way but that wasn't the only reason. We'd been living together for a couple of years.'

He shouldn't have reminded her of that. Living out of wedlock. In sin. What an eejit he is right enough! Will he never learn to stop passing her the ammunition?'

'Have you another woman?' Her voice has dropped an octave. He hears the question that lies behind this one. Are you taking after your father in this way too?

'No, Ma, there's no one,' he says and swallows. There is a lie at the heart of the truth he has just told. And each time he remembers it his throat swells. He puts his fingers to his neck, feels the heat gathering. He cannot tell his mother the whole truth.

'There's still hope, then?'

'For Rachel and me? I doubt it.'

'She was a nice enough girl - I didn't dislike her - but if you'd married one of your own she might have brought you back to the Faith. Brought up your children in the Faith. And what about the two of them? A broken home is the ruination of children, every mortal knows that.'

Can he lay the blame for his ruination at her door, then, hers and his father's? She would say their broken marriage was no fault of hers; his father was the sinner who walked way. There's no point in saying anything, he knows that well enough, so he keeps his mouth closed and makes a face at the wall.

'Holy mother of God,' she keens, 'what did I ever do to deserve this?'

'Nothing, Ma,' he assures her. Except bring him, her only son and child, into the world, a child with strange notions and ambitions who was not content to become a clerk and work for the gas board or sell insurance. She got the length of forty without bearing a child and then something weird must have happened. A virgin birth? He tells himself to give over. If she could hear his thoughts she might have a heart attack. But that could have been her mistake: not to have remained childless, like her four holy sisters. Originally there were six of them, but two had passed away. Not that the remaining ones were that holy; Mary, for a while, until she'd under-gone treatment, was a kleptomaniac, with a notion for bath salts; Sal ran a pub in Dublin; Kathleen in her youth had a long relationship with a married man, a mortician, that ended with the death of his spouse when he upped and married the fancy woman of at least two other men that they knew. Cormac is not aware of any transgressions on the part of Lily, the remaining one of the four, though he has always won-dered about her for she is never out of the confession box. But when it comes to holiness his mother is up front there alongside any of her sisters.

The children are fine, he tells her. Rachel is fine. He is fine. She need not worry though he knows that she will; it is part of her daily life. He has something else to tell her but that will have to wait. The relaying of one piece of bad news is as much as he can cope with in one phone call.

'When are you coming over to see me, son?' she asks, her voice wearied now after her outburst and turning querulous.

'Soon, Ma. As soon as I can.'

'You said you'd come over during the Christmas holidays but you never came. Before that it was the summer holidays.'

'We've had a lot to sort out, what with moving house and all that. I'd better give you my new address and phone number.'

She repeats the words and numbers as she slowly transcribes them, out of his sight. He can see her fingers, though, moving slowly and painfully over the lined pale blue paper. Her hands are arthritic and she's got a touch of it in her knees but there's nothing wrong with her head. She forgets little. Nevertheless, he wonders if he should be thinking about sheltered housing, trying to persuade her. They've got some really nice properties, Ma, well set up, all mod cons, and it'd be your own wee place, with your own furniture and you could suit yourself and there'd be a warden to take care of you if you fell out of bed, answer your bell when you rang. He'd be wasting his breath. The only person for whom she'd toll a bell would be him. She'd say they'd have to take her out in a long box before she'd budge from her own home.

'I'll need to go, I hear someone at the door,' he lies. The afternoon light is waning beyond the window and he has just realised that he is hungry. He'll have to go out and buy something from the nearest Pakistani for their supper. Fish fingers and oven chips. His mother would have a fit if she knew.

'Think about what you're doing, son,' she implores. 'Think about it!'

He is thinking about it, all the time, he tells her, and says goodbye, take care, don't worry, keep warm, make sure you get enough to eat, I'll send you a couple of ten-ners next week, maybe a bit more, but I'm strapped for cash at present, Christmas and all that, you know what it's like, but I'll be over soon.

She says God bless.

Now he has given his mother another sorrow to nurse. He tries to comfort himself with the thought that she likes sorrows, that without them she'd feel bereft.

So there she sits in the little front parlour of her red brick terraced house in Belfast, before a two-barred electric fire with only one bar glowing, the other per-manently dead, to keep the bills down. Her shoulders are slumped under a heavy jumper, knitted before her hands turned rickety, her pale hair pinned tightly back, not one strand straggling, her thin legs encased in opaque greyish stockings that help her veins. Her back is held straight and her head is cocked as she listens to the sound of feet going by in the street. Kids knuckling the glass as they go past. Rattling the letter box. Shouting obscenities through the slot. Causing mayhem. It is not as it was when she was a child. Or when her son was a child. Then the young had respect.

She abides by the ten commandments without diffi-culty. Thou shalt Not Commit Adultery. Thou shalt Not Steal. Thou shalt Not Kill. Oh dear God, how that com-mandment has been transgressed in her province! How many doorsteps in the city have been stained with blood? The man who lived next door to her sister

31

Lily came to the door to answer a knock one night. What a mistake to answer a knock. To take your life in your hands and open your own front door. There was a time when the front doors stood open and the kids played in and out. 'Are you in, Missus?' You trusted even the hawkers to stand in the hallway while you went to get your purse. The man from the Pru would just walk in. Your neighbour came in and out borrowing a half cup of sugar or a few spoons of tea. When you went up the road to the shops you didn't lock the door. Trust. Faith. Hope. All gone.

Now he has depressed himself. What's the point in running through all that old guff in his head? It's not going to change the world.

He opens his front door and looks out into the unfamiliar street. He wonders what Rachel will be doing. Not standing at her door gazing out at the dark, he'll lay a wager on that. She'll be unpacking boxes, hanging up pictures, setting out ornaments, creating a new *home*. She never lies down under adversity. Stop feeling sorry for yourself, boyo! You know that salt smarts in wounds, that it doesn't do anything to heal them. Weren't you told that at your mother's knee? Come on, pick yourself up and stop making a fuss! You were told a lot at your mother's knee right enough and the trouble is it's not easy to forget it.

The houses across the street stand in a regimented row, their staircases lined up in serried ranks, like soldiers on parade. A few lights glow. Lighted windows reassure him. He likes signs of human habitation, is uneasy when he stays too long in country retreats with no other person in sight. What are they doing behind those lit windows? Watching telly. Sleeping off the New Year booze. Playing happy families. Mr Plod the policeman, Mrs Plod and all the little Plods. He wasn't too good at the Plod bit though he loves his children dearly. You're too restless for your own good, Cormac, his mother said, when she had him at her knee.

Above the rooftops, a few stars are coming into the deepening sky. They haven't changed. It's just the bloody earth that has.

He goes inside, calls out again to Davy. 'We'll go and see if we can find a Chinese open. Their New Year's different.'

# Chapter Two

Mornings are not Cormac's best time, unlike his mother who used to be up with the lark, as she termed it, though no larks ever sang in their back yard. He struggles up to quell the alarm, dresses, and prepares his son's breakfast. Davy is no better than he is in the morning.

'Come on, Davy,' he exhorts, 'eat up your egg! And stop messing around.'

'You're not eating anything.'

'I'm not going to school.'

'You're lucky.'

'There's different ways of looking at it.'

'Why aren't you going?' The boy is just stalling, he doesn't really want to know, he senses that it's difficult ground to tread on and he has been only too ready to accept what he was told: that his father has given up teaching to have more time for his sculpture.

'I'm not hungry,' he says finally and pushes the plate away.

'But I made it specially -' Cormac removes the mangled egg. He doesn't know what he's making so much fuss for, he has given Davy his breakfast on numerous occasions, got him ready for school, taken him there. He doesn't have to prove anything, not on that score, anyway.

'Away and get dressed, *pronto*! You don't want to be late. You'll just start the day on the wrong foot.' He puts the dishes in the sink, on top of last night's, and runs hot water on them, to be washed properly later. He hasn't yet adjusted to the idea of no dishwasher. They sold it as a fitment with the house. As Rachel said, neither of them would have room for it in their new kitchens. She has a much more practical outlook on life than he has.

He clears a space on the draining board and quickly makes up two large wholemeal sandwiches, one with cheddar cheese and pickle, the other with peanut butter. That is one thing he is proficient at: making sandwiches. He puts them into a Tupperware box along with an apple and a packet of salt and vinegar crisps.

'Davy!' he calls, putting his head round the door. He can't hear nay movement. He climbs the stairs to find Davy sitting on the bed reading Terry Pratchett. 'Hey, this won't do!' He takes the book from the boy's hands.

'I've got a sore throat.'

'Tell me another one!'

'I have! It's very sore.' He is prone to sore throats. 'You can look if you want to.'

'O.K., I will.' Cormac returns to the kitchen, washes a dessert spoon and rummages amidst the boxes on the floor for his small pocket torch, which cannot be found, and so he settles for the large black rubber one. He goes back up the stairs. 'Right then, open up! Call that open? I can't even get the spoon in.' He places the back of the spoon firmly on Davy's tongue and clicks on the torch. The beam floods Davy's face as well as the cavity of mouth, making him yelp and scrunch up his eyes.

'You're blinding me.'

'Looks perfectly all right to me,' says Cormac, withdrawing the spoon. He hasn't been able to see a thing. 'I'll give you some vitamin C and a drink of orange juice just to make sure.'

'We haven't got any orange juice.'

Cormac makes a mental note to add that to his shopping list. Then he tells Davy to finish dressing, fast! His patience is not elastic. 'You know what happens when a rubber band gets stretched too far.'

Sullenly Davy begins the hunt for socks. 'Can't find two that match,' he announces triumphantly, laying out a red one and a white one with a black and yellow stripe round the top.

'Let me look.' Cormac tips out the contents of a green and white sports bag and picks his way through a heap of washed-out T-shirts, socks and underpants. What a lot of wretched looking garments his son has! How has it come about? He and Rachel are what people would call 'caring parents' (how he dislikes the word!), who have washed their children's clothes regularly, and as far as he is aware, reasonably carefully, even though they didn't always find the time to iron them. He must do something about Davy's wardrobe, if it can be described as such. He will as soon as he gets some extra cash. 'You'll just have to wear two odd socks.'

'Everybody will laugh at me.'

'They won't even see them. Not under your trainers.' Which reminds him: Davy needs a new pair. This lot, although only two months old, look as if they've been kicked through every mud heap in Edinburgh. Davy is kicking mad, like most of his pals. Preferably of footballs. But if none is available any old piece of rubbish will do. The soles of the trainers are beginning to gape. 'Now, listen Davy, I can't take much more of this. So get a move on.'

'My jeans are all scrumpled.'

'Give them to me. I'll put them in the dryer.' Cormac holds out his hand, then remembers that Rachel has taken the dryer, on the grounds that Sophie generates more laundry than anyone else in the family. 'They'll have to do as they are. The heat of your body will help to take out the creases. And don't forget to go to the loo.'

'I hate that loo. It's like sitting in a cupboard under the stairs.'

'It is a cupboard under the stairs.'

Finally, Davy stands, ready for school, clutching his Tupperware box, his feet shod in the disreputable trainers, his backpack sagging from his shoulders, his anorak gaping open, exposing his stomach to whatever winds may blow. He has refused to zip it up, or to put on his woollen hat, for which he has declared outright hatred. Grandma Aherne knitted it for him with her arthritic fingers, though Cormac does not think this is the reason for Davy's dislike. One thing is certain: Grandma Aherne would never have tolerated all this nonsense. Davy would have been in school hours ago, neatly dressed and pressed, with a well scrubbed face, and his breakfast egg inside him.

'Right then, boyo, it's off to work we go!'

Their bicycles take up most of the space in the minute hallway, which makes going in and out something of a problem. Cormac's machine sports two side panniers and a large wicker-covered basket attached to the front handlebars that is handy for shopping. Rachel has the car since she needs it for work. She is a full-time general practitioner.

On opening the door they see that rain has begun to drop from a leaden sky in large gobbets. It looks like being a good downpour but there is no question of waiting for it to go off.

'Put up your hood!' shouts Cormac, as Davy goes bumping down the steps in front of him.

Bulging sacks litter the pavement looking like giant black blisters, alongside sodden cardboard boxes jammed with empty bottles. It is bucket day. Sad looking fir trees sprawl, their branches browning, shedding needles. The end of the old year's garbage. Pity one couldn't clear the rubbish out of one's life as easily, Cormac reflects, and have it taken away in a truck.

They wheel their bicycles across the main road, then they mount to take on the track that the kids call the Snakey which curves upward to the lofty Georgian splendour of Saxe Coburg Place. Davy goes ahead, his bottom high above the saddle, his feet pushing strongly down on the pedals. Cormac finds himself puffing a little. He ought to get in shape, go to a gym or something like that. No, not a gym, he still remembers the awfulness of that at school, not having any talents in that direction. With the start of another new year the newspapers are full of healthy living plans, telling you what to to eat and mostly what you must not (or drink), and which exercises will develop your weaker parts. All his parts feel weak at this time of the day. He always hated nine o'clock classes when he was teaching. He never got quite into his stride until after morning break.

He catches Davy up and in five minutes they reach the school. The puddled playground is deserted except for one or two stragglers dawdling towards the main door. It doesn't seem to matter what time they get into primary school these days. In his era it was almost a hanging matter to arrive after the bell. He was never late; his mother saw to that.

'See you later!' Cormac taps his son on the bottom, hopes that the gesture will not be misconstrued by hidden watchers, watches while the boy stows his bike in the shed, carefully padlocking the front wheel and then flees into school without looking round to wave. Fair enough. Cormac doesn't mind. He didn't look round at his mother, either. His father never took him to school; at this time of day he was intent over his last, working on his shoes, totally absorbed, as intent as any artist. And when he gave that up, in order to better himself and so please his wife, he was away from home much of the week, out on the roads of Ireland, selling shoe polish.

On the way back Cormac goes by a longer, more devious route. He cannot seem to resist it. Of course he could resist anything if he wanted to, couldn't he? That is what Rachel would tell him. He is far too conscious of what other people would tell him. Does it indicate a lack of self-regard?

The playground is empty of people. The teachers' cars are lined up in their allotted places. He recognises most of them, though not a red Citroen. He wonders if it might belong to his successor, a young woman, not long qualified, whom he has heard likes the kind of art that wins the Turner prize. This very moment she might be saying to a class, 'Now take Rodin - or rather,

40

don't take Rodin. He was a tremendous sculptor of course, no one really could deny that, but his approach is old hat nowadays. You want to move forward with the times. You want to start thinking in terms of dead sheep or cow heads in formaldehyde. Shake up the world! That's the artist's role.'

He shook with laughter when the preserved dead sheep came to Edinburgh and the art gallery goers looked round at him as if he was off his head. 'What a con man, eh!' he said to Rachel, who would never let herself get so far out of control as to laugh too loudly in a public place. 'What a brilliant con man! But if people are fool enough to go for it good on him!'

Leaving the school Cormac cycles up to the High Street where he has an errand to do at the City Chambers, then decides to have a coffee before starting work. The city is bristling with new coffee houses offering cappuccino and cafe latte and croissants plain, almond, or au chocolat. He took up the cafe habit after his suspension, working his way round a large and varied selection. He had to do something, he'd have gone clean off his rocker if he'd sat in the house all day watching old films, and he couldn't bear to go up to his studio at the top of the house. The piece he'd been working on before he went to Paris had gone dead on him. Nearly every aspect of his life had died a death. His marriage, friendships. He avoided friends to spare them their embarrassment. Whenever he passed someone he vaguely knew he'd suspect they suspected him, were pointing the finger. *Look, there he is! The one who? Yes, the one! That's him!* Chinese whispers creeping along the streets, swelling to an uproar. *That's him! The*

41

*monster! To think that a man like him was in charge of our children!* He knew that even hardened criminals abhorred child abusers, gave them a hard time in prison. During broken nights when he rose from the marital bed sweating at the thought of being incarcerated, an outcast from society, any kind of society, he'd descend to the kitchen where he'd open the back door and stand gulping in the night air until the terror passed.

He puts thoughts of such nights behind him and cycles on down the Royal Mile. He brakes outside a cafe called Clarinda's. Why does he do this to himself? He is not sure. He tells himself that this establishment, being along the lines of an old-fashioned type of tearoom with scones and apple tart (he has been here before, more than once), has an appeal after so much chrome and fizzy milk and cries of short-semi-caffe latte. He tells himself, too, that he has no need to run away from a cafe simply because it bears a particular name. He goes in and sits at a table with a lacy-edged cloth and orders straight black coffee.

Clarinda's mother is a Burns fan. She is passionate about the poet; hence the naming of her one and only child. Burns' Clarinda in real life had been a Mrs Agnes McLehose, a widow woman, but Mrs Bain would have ignored that. She took what she wanted out of any situation. The name Clarinda would have suggested romance to her and that was enough. She has a photograph of the poet on top of her piano and another on her bedside table. She recites one of his poems every night before she goes to sleep. You could say she was obsessed, Clarinda told him, laughing. She knew that Cormac was interested in other people's obsessions.

She was his most attentive pupil in class, the most ardent.

He was talking about Rodin. At the end of the afternoon, in the dying moments of his last class of the day, which tended to be one of his older classes, he sometimes talked about the sculptor and showed slides of his work. He always felt relaxed when he got on to his pet subject; it was like coming home. He could start to unwind.

When he looked up from the slide projector he saw that Clarinda Bain was listening intently, elbows propped on desk, her face resting in the cup of her hands, framed by her pale shoulder-length hair. She sat very still in class compared to most of the others who tended to wriggle and twitch and shift on their seats and her eyes, a deep, intense blue bordering on violet, framed by exceptionally long dark lashes, held a level gaze when studying an object or a person. When talking to the class he often found himself looking in her direction. One tended to look at the pupils who were the most responsive so that one felt encouraged to go on. She was one of the high flyers in her year, referred to as 'bright' by members of staff in all departments, a bit of a loner, not in with a crowd, which seemed not to trouble her.

He looked back at the screen, at the image reflected on it of the bust of a young woman with head inclined and eyes closed.

'This is *Le Sommeil,*' he said, 'one of Rodin's most tender pieces. Can you see how soft and sensual her face is? You won't be able to appreciate his work fully until we go to Paris and you see it in the flesh. That's what it feels like when you stand in front of one of his sculptures: you feel you can see the flesh that inspired him.'

At the mention of flesh one of the two boys at the back who had appeared to be asleep roused themselves to ask if anything but sex and women had inspired Rodin. Somebody whistled. The boy who had asked the question was a Damien Hirst fan and unlikely to be converted to Cormac's own passion but he was himself quite a promising artist while lacking that commitment that would lift him into another sphere. He was young, though, Cormac had to remind himself of that when tempted to judge his pupils too harshly.

'Nature inspired him, and life itself,' he responded, though he had to admit that it was true that Rodin had been obsessed by women and their sexuality. His sculptures demonstrated that fully and gloriously.

'Would you call them erotic?' asked a boy called Jason, tongue in cheek, as Cormac was aware. Jason had brought in a piece of work decorated with dog shit on one occasion and had pretended indignation when asked to remove it. 'What about those pictures daubed with elephant shit? They were hung in a gallery.' Cormac had said that the ordure of elephants obviously could not smell as strongly as that of dogs.

'Or pornographic,' put in Robbie, the Damien Hirst fan and then answered himself. 'It might be if it was on page three, mightn't it?'

Cormac inclined his head, acknowledging his point.

'Do you think an artist's personality is reflected in his work?' asked Clarinda, frowning a little.

'What do you think?' Cormac asked the class.

'I reckon it was with Jason's dog shit,' said Robbie,

which caused some laughter and meant that he had to duck out of Jason's range.

'I think we could say that Rodin's personality is reflected in his work,' said Cormac, bringing them back to the central topic, though he enjoyed it when their discussions wandered off at tangents. 'He was a very passionate and sensual man. His work is charged with emotion and energy, you can tell that even seeing it here on the screen, two-dimensionally.'

'Did he have it off with his models then?' asked Robbie.

'As a matter of fact, yes, he usually did.'

The room was warm, the discussion genial. Cormac felt in good form and was not even riled when one of the boys asked him if he had any other heroes but Rodin, making him sound like a football follower.

'Don't you feel a need to move on?'

'I hope I have moved on in that I have looked at other things and I admire many of them though I do confess - without shame! - that I find it difficult when it comes to sculpture to go past Rodin. To my mind he is the king.' Cornac left school that afternoon feeling buoyant, to walk home. Teaching got a bad press but he enjoyed it, most of the time. He'd had a good afternoon.

He sometimes thought he had better conversations with his students than he did when he and Rachel went to dinner parties, especially those given by colleagues of his or hers. They talked about Edinburgh restaurants and foreign holidays. He and Rachel usually went to southern Europe, to France, Italy or Spain, and so could not compare notes on Bangkok, Bali or Copocabana Beach.

Turning a corner, on his way home, he bumped into Clarinda. At the time that was what he thought: that he had bumped into her, that their meeting was accidental. Later, while walking the streets and sitting in cafes, a suspended man, ruminating over his fate, he would come to wonder if she had been waiting for him that day and other days.

'I really enjoy your classes, Mr Aherne,' she said.

He was pleased, even flattered, for who would not be pleased when receiving praise from a pupil? The pupils were the ones that mattered most, after all, not the dreary inspectors who came and sat at the back of the class trying to look benign.

'I do think Rodin's wonderful, too. I've only seen your slides and photographs of course and I know they won't be anything like the real thing. I can't wait to get to Paris!'

Cormac smiled. He had felt like that on the brink of his first trip. His mother had not been happy about him going off to the French capital on his own even though he had been eighteen years old and about to go to art college in Edinburgh. She had not been happy about that, either, of course not. What did he want to go to Edinburgh for when there was a perfectly good college in Belfast and he could live more cheaply at home?

'It's great to be young,' he told Clarinda, 'and to be looking at things for the very first time.'

Hearing the trill of a bicycle bell, he glanced round to see Alec McCaffy, teacher of geography, his ankles firmly clipped, mounted on his high bicycle. No mountain bike this, it looked like something Les's father might have left in the back shed before popping off. Les still lived in his childhood home, with his mother.

'Oh hi, Alec,' muttered Cormac offhandedly and turned back to Clarinda.

She said, 'I'd love to read something about Rodin.'

'I'll bring in a couple of books for you,' he promised, glancing at his watch. 'I must go. I've got to collect my son from the childminder's.'

After he'd brought Davy home and given him his customary afternoon refreshment he went up to his studio and looked out some books on Rodin and his times. He gave them a dust. He had read them more than once in times past, when life had been more leisurely. He opened one book and the next thing he knew was Rachel calling from below, 'Are you in, Cormac?'

He ran downstairs. She was taking off her coat in the hall. She looked tired.

'How was your day?' he asked.

'Hellish. I thought I'd never got out of the surgery and when I did I had two emergency house calls. One died before I got there. I could do with a drink.'

He poured her a gin and tonic and took a dram for himself. They had the living room to themselves. Sophie wasn't back yet and Davy was watching television in his room. They had succumbed to buying a set for him in order to get a bit of peace for themselves. Not a worthy reason, they had both acknowledged, but they were full-time working people with fairly stressful jobs and they needed all the help they could get.

Rachel sighed. 'That feels better. How was your day?'

'Great,' he said.

Next morning, in the staff room, waiting side by side for the kettle to boil for their Nescafe, Alec McCaffy said, 'You seemed to be having quite a jaw-jaw with Miss Clarinda Bain on the corner there yesterday afternoon. She was hanging onto your every word.'

'We were discussing art,' said Cormac loftily, lifting the steaming kettle and pouring hissing water onto the brown powder in his mug. 'In particular, Rodin and his sculpture, in preparation for our visit to Paris.'

'I wasn't suggesting you were talking about anything else,' said Les, with a little smirk that Cormac did not much care for.

For God's sake all he had been doing was talking to a pupil about his subject, in full view, on a corner! She was interested in art, this girl, passionate about it, which he could understand and relate to and he couldn't help it if some of his colleagues wouldn't know what the word passion meant. As for Alec McCaffy, staleness came off him and his bicycle clips like bad breath.

He saw Clarinda in the corridor and told her that he had brought some books for her. 'Come and see me at the end of the day.'

His last class on this day was a fourth year group whom he found dispiriting. At least half of them couldn't wait to leave school at the end of the year and were taking art, thinking it to be a soft option. They made nuisances of themselves splashing paint about and generally disrupting the concentration of the class which meant that Cormac had to be constantly sniping at them. He was delighted to see the back of them and pleased to see Clarinda coming in the door with an eager face.

He took the books from his bag and laid them on the table in front of her.

'You can dip into some of these.'

'Fantastic!'

He wondered if any of Alec McCaffy's pupils had ever pronounced anything to be fantastic in a class of his.

Clarinda opened one of the books and began to study the plates. 'Looking at these makes me want to get on and do something.'

The door opened at their backs and his friend Ken Mason put his head in. 'Oh, you're busy, Cormac.' He was about to withdraw.

'No, it's all right. I'm just coming.' He'd promised to go for a drink with Ken.

Clarinda was gathering up the books. 'Thank you very much for these, Mr Aherne,' she said and clutching them to her bosom, left them.

'Keen student?' asked Ken.

'Very keen.'

'You can be such a fool at times, Cormac, like an innocent abroad!' Rachel told him on the day he arrived home to tell her that he had been suspended. Sent home like a recalcitrant schoolboy by the headmaster. He had been sent home once before, when he was a pupil in primary school, for telling a teacher that he liked her blouse. You could see her bra through the gauzy material. The other boys put him up to it. 'Go on, Cormie, tell her!' 'What did I do wrong, sir?' he asked the headmaster. 'It's a nice blouse.' He was told not to to be cheeky and to hold out his hand. Then he was sent home to consider his sin. His mother took the headmaster's side.

So once again, here he was, considering. Some people never learnt. They were standing in the kitchen, he and Rachel, and Davy was upstairs in his room watching television with the sound turned up too high, which, for once, had its advantage. Rachel had come in only a minute ahead of Cormac and had not even had time to take off her coat when he'd blurted out his news. She was resting her back against the counter top as if her legs were too weak to hold her up. Cormac ran the cold tap and took a long drink. It soured his mouth to think that Archie Gibson had offered no word of support even after they'd concluded the formal part of the proceedings. He'd stopped at the door of his room to give him the opportunity but he'd been hunched over his desk with blank eyes writing a report for some damn fool bureaucrat. That legion of nit-pickers and snoopers that polluted the land. Cormac had seen Archie's eyes flicker but he hadn't looked up. So much for friendship. He took another drink of water. And now here was his wife calling him a fool.

'Oh, I'm sorry, Cormac,' she said with a sigh, heaving herself off the counter. 'I didn't mean it, really I didn't.'

'Yes, you did. And perhaps I am.'

She gave her head a quick shake as if to settle what was going on inside it. 'It was just - well, it was a shock, damn it all! And you're so impulsive always. You never stop to think and as a result you leave yourself exposed. You'd think you might have learned to protect yourself a bit better by this time.'

She was not by nature a harsh woman, except in odd moments, when she was exasperated as well as distressed. And this was one of them. She had been taken completely by surprise and so had spoken what was in her mind, without thinking. He didn't doubt that any woman would be upset to hear that her husband had been accused of making sexual advances to a minor, a pupil in his care, and might even entertain a grain of doubt about his innocence. And what she had to say was true, about protecting himself. Putting up a guard. Covering his flanks. As in war. His trouble was that he was too spontaneous by nature and that on occasions had infuriated her. Like the time when they'd met some people on holiday in Greece (exceedingly boring as well as greedy people, said Rachel, telling the tale to friends afterwards) and he'd said casually that they were welcome to come and stay with them in Edinburgh and they did, two adults and two gargantuan teenagers, for ten whole days of the Festival in August, treating their house like a free B&B, expecting an evening meal thrown in to which they contributed a cheap bottle of Bulgarian plonk that Rachel saw priced at one pound ninety nine p. in a supermarket. 'Why *don't* you think, Cormac, before you open your mouth?' she asked after the freeloaders had departed. It was always said that he was like his father in that respect, as well as being good with his hands. That was his mother's term for it.

His father had been an ebullient man and liked a good laugh. He had a repertoire of jokes. 'Have you heard the one about the man coming to the funeral, knocking on the door and asking, "Is this where the dead man lives?" He'd throw his head back and laugh till his wife left the room shaking her head. He liked a drink as well, did Pat Aherne, nothing wrong with that for he never drank too much or came home stotious, swearing and falling all over the place and beating up his wife and child, like some, like their next-door neighbour who was a Salvationist when sober. Pat Aherne liked the company as much as the beer and was known in the pub to be good crack.

He gave up the shoemaking since he was an obliging man and his wife thought he could do better for himself, and her. He got a job as a commercial traveller, later to be known as a sales representative, and thereafter he sold shoe polish the length and breadth of Ireland. He liked travelling the country, meeting people, and he liked staying in the cheap bacon-and-egg hotels and bed-and-breakfasts run by soft-bosomed women. It was great, he told his son, getting bacon and egg and fried potato bread set in front of you every morning and no one wanting to nag at you! He got a car, too, and on Sundays he'd take his wife and child and one or two of his wife's sisters for runs down the coast to Bangor and Donaghadee. The women would sit gossiping in the car while he and the boy kicked a football and built castles on the beach, sculpting the sand carefully, building it up piece by piece, until they could sit back on their hunkers and admire their handiwork. Their work of art. They never jumped on it to flatten the pile. 'Let the sea take it when it's ready,' said Cormac's father. 'The main thing is to have built the castle.'

By this time the women would be getting restless and Cormac's mother would have wound down her window and be calling out, 'Are the two of youse not done yet? It's getting chilly.' To cheer them up Pat would buy them all ice cream sliders and the aunts would curl their tongues round the edge of the ices to stop them dripping on their Sunday clothes and say, 'You're in the money, Pat!' 'Not that much!' his wife would retaliate sharply. It was all very well for him to be so open-handed and buy ice creams all round, not to mention standing rounds in the pub but, at the end of the day, it was she who would have to make ends meet.

At the end of the day, Cormac's father disappeared. He didn't come home one Friday afternoon as usual.

'There'll be a woman involved,' said his Aunt Lily knowingly. 'You can take my word for it! There usually is.'

His mother had feared that her son might grow up in the image of his father. He heard her say to her sister Lily in the kitchen one day that maybe it was as well his father had done a bunk. 'He'd have been a bad influence on the boy so he would.'

'Cormac, I was talking to you.' Rachel's voice had softened. 'Don't think you heard me though, did you?'

He blinked. His wife was regarding him quizzically. She had taken off her coat and was sitting at the kitchen table. She looked tired. She'd probably had a hard day at work and the last thing she needed was trouble at home.

'What did you say the girl's name was?'

He did not recall saying. 'Clarinda Bain,' he said now with some difficulty.

'What age is she exactly?'

'Sixteen.'

'Thank goodness for that! At least she's past the age of consent.'

'She was only fifteen when we were in Paris.'

'Oh *no*!'

'She had her sixteenth birthday the day after we came back.'

'That won't be taken into account.'

'When I am called to account? Rachel, I want you to know that I did not attempt to seduce her.'

'It's terrible that you should be suspended on her say-so.'

'It's the rules.'

'Oh, I know Archie wouldn't have done it if he could have avoided it. But what evidence do the Bains have?'

'None, except Clarinda's word. But that is enough. A word from her. And one from her mother.' He groaned at the thought of her mother. She would not be a reluctant witness in the box, she'd let her imagination take wing and soar into orbit.

'What are we to tell Sophie? Fourteen is a such a difficult age, especially for coping with something like this. At least Davy's too young for it to impinge on him.'

'What will other people think?' said Cormac, his voice edged with sarcasm which Rachel did not appear to be registering. 'No smoke, you know.'

'It's not going to be very amusing, certainly.'

'No, not exactly a laugh a minute. I'll be tarnished.' He wondered if he should scrub his hands until they were pink and raw and clean. Clean hands, clean heart. His heart didn't feel clean; it felt murderous. Towards Archie Gibson, which was not rational, and Clarinda Bain, which was.

'Clarinda Bain,' said Rachel. 'Wasn't she the pretty fair-haired girl who played Ophelia in the school play last year? Good actress.'

'Yes, she should do well in the witness box.' *Witness box?* Was all of this real? He still had the feeling of being caught up in a nightmare that must surely end with the coming of daylight. But no matter which way he turned he could see no light.

'She looked very mature for her age.'

'They all do these days.' He patted his pocket then remembered that he had given up smoking a couple of years ago. Sophie's nagging had made him give up as much as anything else. She had threatened to leave home for a cleaner environment if he did not.

'I suppose,' said Rachel, then stopped.

'Suppose what?'

'Well, you didn't ...? No, I'm sure you wouldn't.'

'Oh good, I'm glad you have faith in me.'

'She couldn't have, well, misread the signals?'

'What bloody signals? I don't give out *signals*, dammit, I'm not a transmitter, I *talk* to my pupils, I try to educate them. That's my job. *Was* my job.'

'All right, no need to go on! It's just, knowing you -'

'Do you?'

'For God's sake, Cormac, let me finish!'

'So what do you wish to say about knowing me?'

'It's just that you might have put your arm round her in a fatherly sort of way and she might have misinterpreted that. You are a very tactile person, aren't you?'

'I can't help being tactile. It's the way I am. You like me touching you, don't you?'

'I'm your wife, Cormac. But she -'

'We are strictly forbidden to lay a finger on our pupils. Sometimes you forget and you put a hand on their shoulders. You might even brush against them, inadvertently. Don't you ever touch your patients?'

'Of course I do, when I examine them. It's part of my job, and that is understood.'

'But don't you ever want to lay a hand on them in a purely reassuring way? Don't you ever want to say to them, "It's going to be all right?"'

'Sometimes I might but I'm conscious that there's a thin dividing line between what is admissible and what is not. I'm very careful, always.'

'I'm sure you are. Bloody careful! You'd never act without thinking, would you?'

'I have to be careful. I'd be struck off I weren't. But don't take it out on me, please, Cormac! It's not my fault.'

There it was: the first crack in their marriage. Not true, of course: with temperaments as diverse as theirs there had inevitably been small cracks and fissures over the years, but they had mostly healed or been plastered over so that the ruptures did not show, except in times of stress.

Rachel yawned suddenly, allowing a wave of tiredness to sweep over her. She stood up. They looked at each other, then he opened his arms to her and she moved into them, letting her head fall against his shoulder. He rested his face in her hair. 'It's going to be all right,' he wanted to tell her, but the words would not come.

# Chapter Three

On leaving Clarinda's tea shop Cormac unlocks his bicycle and cycles back across Princes Street, stopping off to buy two litres of milk which he stows in his wicker basket. The rest of his shopping he did the night before. He finds it a boon that one can shop at all hours of the day and night.

He opens up his shop. *Cormac's Carry-Outs*. Come and get them freshly cut! When he started he put leaflets through the letter boxes of various companies in the area. This is his little empire. Here, he can do whatever he wishes. He has freedom of choice. He can make tuna sandwiches with raspberries, smoked mackerel with cream cheese, pork with anchovy, should it take his fancy, which it doesn't particularly. He doesn't have to be answerable to anyone but his customers. And if they don't like what he has on offer they can go elsewhere. The sandwich business is booming. They have grown up around the city like mushrooms. *Quick Bites. Better Bites. Food for Thought.* And so on, and on. Sometimes there's just the owner's name. Quite a few of the names are Irish, Cormac has noted, and is not sure what to make of that. That the Irish are good at making sandwiches or that they're more often desperate and on their uppers?

His mother would go mad if she saw his name emblazoned above a shop selling sandwiches.

So now, instead of nurturing young minds, putting ideas into their heads that won't lead to secure jobs in the Scottish Office or Scottish Widows, he is feeding the bellies of the citizens of Edinburgh, the bank and insurance clerks, the legal secretaries, the lawyers, the hairdressers and psychotherapists, the slaters and steeple jacks, the road diggers, the traffic wardens, the policemen who pull up in their squad cars on the double yellow line, the occasional housewife who wants to eat someone else's sandwiches for a change. He gets all kinds. It takes all kinds to put enough money through the till, to fill his belly and that of his son. He is not prepared to be subsidised by his wife. Or ex-wife, as she really is, even though they are not divorced. She offered, but he refused.

He goes through to the kitchen at the back and lays bacon in neat rashers under the grill. BLT is always popular, as is tuna mayonnaise and coronation chicken, though he does do a few more esoteric mixtures using avocados and Chinese gooseberries. He takes the ingredients for today's fillings out of the fridge, which is everything in the fridge. When Rachel finishes work he will borrow the car and go to Cash and Carry and stock up again.

Selina, his help, arrives. She is a former student, one that did listen to his talk. She is a painter and likes to paint predominantly in oil on large canvases. None of her friends can afford them. She comes in stripping herself of various garments to reveal her usual black garb of black leggings and black t-shirt. She has rings in her ears and rings in her nose and perhaps in other places, too, for all Cormac knows. He is glad that, so far, Sophie has shown no sign of getting pierced. One of her friends got her tongue done and it went septic; he thinks, hopes, that may have put Sophie off.

They set to work and by eleven o'clock have laid out on the shelves their offerings of bread sandwiches, on brown, white and rye, and various shapes, sizes and types of rolls, all tidily wrapped in cling film. Cormac takes satisfaction in the presentation of his sandwiches; he wants each one to look perfectly cut, yes, sculpted. When he sets them out he likes to be able to think, I cannot improve on this, they are everything anyone could wish. When he used to complete a piece of sculpture he would think, it lacks an element, it needs something more, it is not as perfect as I would have wished, as I anticipated, as it was as a concept in my head. 'So, you see,' he says to Selina, 'there is great aesthetic satisfaction to be derived from working in a sandwich bar. And much less trauma than trying to produce a work of art.'

'You could talk your way round anything, Cormac,' says Selina. 'You remind me of my mother's Uncle Gerry. He was Irish too.'

They stand behind the counter with their handiwork on show, awaiting customers. They begin to trickle in, without fail, which is another aspect that Cormac appreciates. There is no suspense, no waiting to see if anyone will come, as he has had to do in the past when he had a show. And even then, half of those who did come would turn their backs on the exhibits - his creations - and chat to other inveterate exhibition-goers whilst downing as much free wine as they could lay hands on. Those who come into his shop come for one purpose only: to purchase sandwiches. The main flood comes normally between twelve and one-thirty, then it dwindles to a dribble again.

At half-past two, Gentleman Jock pays them his daily visit in his long tattered overcoat with the newspaper stuffed down the front. He pushes an old bicycle with flat tires and broken spokes; from its twisted handle-bars hang an assortment of old carrier bags. He is one of the old homeless, not the new, who are to be seen dotted at regular intervals along Princes Street with their dogs and pieces of cardboard saying HOMELESS AND HUNGRY. Jock has been on the road for more years than he can remember, though once he worked in a hotel, had a good job, accommodation provided, was working up to be head porter, and then he had a nervous breakdown, and that had more or less been that.

'What do you fancy today then, Jock?' asks Cormac. 'Cheese and pickle? Smoked chicken and salad?'

Jock fancies anything as long as it is edible. He waits on the pavement while Cormac goes to fetch the food. He would never make a move to come inside or expect to be asked. He understands. Nevertheless, Cormac feels badly that he never does ask him to come through to the back kitchen and warm himself. Who does he think he is? Lord Muck doling out hand-outs and feeling pleased with himself? But take care not to pollute my cosy little world! Do not step over the mark. Bloody hypocrisy. 'But he stinks,' says Selina. 'The place would smell like a doss house afterwards. You'd lose customers. You might have to close. You'd be out of work. And so would I.' In spite of having listened to him during her formative years she is sensible, sharp and street-wise. He makes a mental note to bring in a pair of thick hiking socks for the old fella.

At three, Cormac has to go, to leave Selina to do the final clearing up. He jumps back on his bike and heads for the school playground where he joins the gaggle of mothers and grandmothers and the occasional father and grandfather clustered round the gate.

The phone is ringing as they come in. Davy drops his bags and goes ahead to answer it.

'Oh, hi, Grandma!' he says. 'We were at the Cash and Carry. You know, where you get cheap stuff. For Dad's sandwiches. He thought he'd best get it today even though he doesn't open on Saturdays, so he'll be all set for Monday.'

Cormac can imagine his mother's reaction at the other end of the line. '*Sandwiches*, Davy? What sandwiches?'

'For his sandwich bar. He makes all kinds. I like BLT the best.'

'Better give me the phone.' Cormac holds out his hand.

'You're working in a *sandwich* bar,' says his mother, her incredulity travelling across the Irish sea. What an amazing thing science is, Cormac reflects, and what a damned nuisance it can be too. Oh for the days when letters went to and fro bobbing about on the waves taking days, weeks, to reach their targets. Or perhaps, if one was lucky, going soggy on the sea crossing, and sinking without trace.

'I'm not working in one, Ma. It's mine. I'm the proprietor.'

'What *is* a sandwich bar? she demands to know. Of course she is out of touch with modern life. How could she not be sitting there in her terraced house, leaving it only to venture to the corner shop and the church? Sandwich bars don't touch her life, God may be praised for that.

'A place that sells sandwiches,' he explains patiently. 'It's got nothing to do with a pub. I only sell orange and apple juice in cartons and Coca-Cola, Seven-Up and Irn Bru in tins.'

'You're running one of these things? When I think -'

'I know, I know!' He can follow her thoughts. She will be relishing the memory of every sacrifice, every cream bun passed over, every holiday not taken, so that he could get a good education. And then he went to Art College! He might have been better leaving school at sixteen and learning a trade. He could have had his own plumbing business by now and be driving a BMW. But he is being too cynical. She's a decent woman, after all. And it's indecent of him to be lampooning her, even in his head. She's got courage and nerve and holds steady to her beliefs, qualities not to be dismissed. And she brought him up, fed him and cared for him. He sighs and says he's sorry.

'But why aren't you at the school?' When he went into teaching, giving way, on marriage, to realism, she thought he had come to his senses. 'You never got the sack, did you?'

He is only half listening. He has been thinking about Rachel on their wedding day, her dark head sleek under a white veil - both mothers had been so happy that it had been a proper church wedding with all the trimmings, even though the bride was five months pregnant - and how she looked up at him with her calm grey eyes and agreed to take him on for better or

62

worse. He thought then that there was no way this bond between them could ever be rent asunder.

'*Did* you get the sack, Cormac?'

'No, Ma, nothing like that. I just decided to leave.'

'To *leave*? Don't you realise how lucky you were to be having such a good job? And to exchange it for a *sandwich bar*!'

'I always liked cooking,' he says defensively. 'It's creative.' And easier than sculpture, he adds, and more lucrative, but too quietly for her to hear.

'Making sandwiches is not what I'd call cooking!'

He remembers hers as white-breaded, triangular, daintily cut, and crustless, with thin fillings of fish paste, egg and cress, ham, and something called sandwich spread which was a kind of salad cream with bits in it. The sandwiches rested on snowy white doilies and were served up when the priest or her sisters came to call. Cormac tells her that sandwiches are a different affair entirely these days; they're hearty, offered up on long slices of baguette or in thick Italian rolls, and bursting with filling. He rattles off a list of fillings, hoping to stun her into silence, or perhaps even impress her. Tuna mayonnaise, coronation chicken, brie and lettuce, smoked salmon and cream cheese, Stilton and celery, ham and pineapple, turkey and avocado, BLT - At that she stops him in his tracks, demanding to know what BLT means.

'Bacon, lettuce and tomato. Very popular. Mine is an up market sandwich bar, Ma. No greasy fried egg rolls for my customers.'

'Who buys these sandwiches of yours?'

'The hungry. Working men and women.'

'Why don't they bring their sandwiches with them

from home? It doesn't take a minute to spread a piece of bread and put a filling in. Any fool could do that. They must have money to burn. Or else they're too lazy, more like.'

'Convenience food, Ma. It's a new age.' She sighs. 'It's time I was away.' Her voice goes down like a gas flame dwindling to a peep.

'Come on now, Ma, there's plenty life in you yet.'

Silence. He thinks he can hear the waves sloshing.

'Are you all right, Ma?' He rattles the receiver rest.

'How can I be all right?' It is barely a whisper.

'Will Aunt Lily be coming over to see you?'

'Lily has her own life to lead. She has her own friends.'

'Well, listen, just you hang in there and I ...' This is a repeat message. 'Ma, are you listening? Are you?'

The next day being Saturday, it is his turn to have Sophie, and for Davy to go to his mother. The boy goes eagerly, getting up at the first call, dressing swiftly and packing his overnight bag without being chivvied. Cormac tries not to feel depressed. Sophie, by contrast, when she arrives, shows no sign of eagerness. She can't stop yawning and when he asks her what she would like to do she lifts one shoulder in a shrug. To make anything of the day they need an uplift and so he decides to take her out for lunch to a small French bistro in the old town, even though he can't really afford it. That's you all over, Cormac, his mother would say. Oh shut up, Ma, he says silently, can't you let me get me on with my own life!

They walk up to Princes Street, cutting across the stream of Saturday shoppers that eddies and flows along it carrying multitudes of carrier bags. The new leisure activity, Cormac murmurs. New since he was a boy, he means. He and his mother went downtown only when he *needed* a new blazer or school shoes. Nowadays, the shoppers are out even on Sundays thronging the malls and carpet warehouses. Shopping has replaced Sunday worship, he comments, as they wait in the middle of a restless group for the red man to change to green. It is an activity that can be done *en famille*.

'It's disgusting,' says Sophie in a loud voice. 'Spending all that money when half the world is starving. It's not as if they need all those things.'

That draws a few dirty looks from those around them. Fortunately the light changes at this point and they all surge forward. Cormac is surprised himself by Sophie's remark. It wasn't long ago that she was out with everyone else on a Saturday rummaging for cheap earrings and eye liner and the latest hit single, spending every penny she could lay hands on, trying to cadge more when she came home. He notices that she is not wearing eye make-up today and is dressed in some long woollen garment that has seen brighter days. She must have entered a new phase. Surely not in the two weeks they've been living apart! Can she have changed that quickly? Or has he been so preoccupied with his own affairs that he hasn't even noticed? He is cheered, however, to know that Sophie is developing a social conscience. The young are so materialistic now, compared with when he was a student. A pompous thought, but he can't help thinking it. It's not their fault: they are products of the market economy.

They pass along by the side of the art gallery and

come to the steep rise of the Playfair steps which will take them up to the shoulder of the Mound. As usual there is a grubby young man sitting at the foot of the steps guarded by some sort of German wolf hound slavering unpleasantly between yellow teeth. Cormac has never been fond of dogs since one bit him on the calf where he was a boy. He is an urban man, likes streets and lights and people, and feels that animals have no place in the city fouling its pavements and green spaces. The path along the Water of Leith is littered with dog turds for children to slip and slide on, mess up their hands with, and infect their eyes. Recently a boy, after falling on dog shit on the riverside pathway, has gone blind. Cormac wonders how this young man manages to feed the dog, though not out loud, for Sophie would certainly counter with a quick attack.

'Give him something, Dad,' she says.

He tosses a twenty p. coin into the young man's cap.

'Give him some more,' she urges. 'Twenty p. is nothing.'

He throws down a pound coin and the young man winks at Sophie. He has a rather distinctive mark below his left eye. Looking closer, Cormac sees that it is a birthmark shaped like a kite. He puts a proprietorial hand under his daughter's elbow, not that she would be likely to need his protection. She would probably be readier than he to deliver a swift kick to the man's shins should he become obnoxious. They begin their ascent of the steps.

'That doesn't solve the problem, you know,' he says.

'I'm aware of that.'

'Some of them could get jobs if they tried.'

'They could always open sandwich bars. If they had the dosh.'

He makes no reply. It would be too boring to pursue the conversation. And he doesn't want to have any arguments with his daughter on the one day in the week that they spend together. This is supposed to be what is known as 'quality time'. Another phrase that makes him shudder.

They reach the High Street and turn down the narrow Fishmonger's Close, watching their feet on the cobblestones slippery with bird shit. He loves the mediaeval old town, would have liked to have lived in it if it were not for the children and their schools. He likes the closed-in feeling of the streets, its areas of secret darkness, and the way the buildings huddle together, whereas Rachel prefers the space and light of the Georgian New Town. It was amazing that they had ever got on together, and yet not. Their recognition of each other was immediate and explosive, a meeting of minds and bodies. He remembers it vividly, the sudden wonder of it, the laughter, their inability to let go of each other. And now ... He almost slips and is saved by Sophie's hand.

'Thanks, my love. I always knew a daughter would come in useful one day.'

The bistro, which is housed in a seventeenth century building, lies at the foot of the alleyway. The low-ceilinged rooms are bustling and cheerful with the sound of talk and clink of glasses and cutlery and Cormac is delighted to be taking his daughter out to lunch. He holds her chair.

'Can you afford this?' she asks, peeling off her mittens and unwinding two long woollen scarves from around her neck. 'Are sandwiches selling like hot cakes?'

'Sure! No problem.'

He orders a bottle of house red with their food.

'Will you have a glass?' He doesn't need to ask. She has two glasses, might have three if she were given the chance. But she is only fifteen. She leans her elbows on the table. She becomes talkative. She talks of going to Greece, of wandering from island to island. All normal teenage stuff. Dreams of freedom, casting off the parental shackles. Cormac is reassured. Rachel was saying that Sophie has been behaving oddly and playing hookey from school. She asked him to try to find out what Sophie is up to. 'She talks to you more than to me,' said Rachel.

'How's school?' he asks.

She wrinkles her nose. 'It's so cut off.'

'From what?'

'The real world.'

He could start up a little homily on the value of education but decides against it. She knows what he thinks on the subject, anyway. And he is less sure about the value of anything now. What has it ever done for you? she might ask. Look at you, forty-four years old, all that taxpayers' money spent on you, and there you are making sandwiches which any fool could do. You might as well have left school at sixteen. You might have worked your way up to owning a chain of sandwich bars by this time with other people doing the cutting and slicing.

'How's your mother?' he asks casually.

'Seems O.K. Busy. She's always busy, isn't she, with all her committees and whatnot? As if she's afraid to stop.'

They have finished the wine. Cormac turns to catch

the waiter's eye and catches the eye of Clarinda Bain instead.

The police came to interview him the day after he was suspended. Two constables arrived, a man and a woman. He felt the woman's aggression the moment he opened the door; it hit him like a slap in the face with a wet cloth. It was the first of many such looks he would encounter.

'Cormac Aherne?'

He admitted his identity.

'May we come in?'

He held open the door. He was prepared to co-operate; it would be foolish not to. He'd do anything to get out of this hell-hole that he had been dropped into. Anything? That remained to be seen.

'Look,' he said to the constables as soon as they'd taken off their hats and seated themselves side by side on the pale blue leather settee that he and Rachel had purchased just before he'd taken off for Paris. Paris! His favourite city! Would he ever be able to go there again? 'Look,' he said again, extending his hand, appealing to them, 'this whole business has got out of proportion.'

It was not for them to make any judgment on that; a complaint had been made against him by a minor, of a serious nature. She was not a minor now, he pointed out. But she was then, they retaliated. By a week, he countered futilely, but all this was just by way of being a red herring, of playing for time that was not available.

'Can I just say that I did not attempt to seduce her!'

'She claims that you did.'

'She bloody well made advances to me.'

The policewoman looked at him stonily. Did he

expect her to believe that? That a fifteen-year-old pupil would try to seduce her forty-four-year-old teacher who was already sporting a number of grey hairs and who was carrying more weight than when he was in his prime?

'I'm not the first poor sod to be dumped in the shit like this,' he told them. 'It's happened before. You must read the papers?' *Careful now, Cormac.* He could hear Rachel's voice in his ear. *Don't say anything that will antagonise them further.*

They were perfectly polite, he couldn't complain about that. They asked him to come down to the station with them and make a statement.

'You'll get your chance to put your side of the story then,' said the male constable.

'So it'll be my word against hers?'

'Unless there are witnesses,' said the woman.

'Witnesses?'

'Other pupils. Teachers.'

He thought of Alec McCaffy, the teacher who had accompanied him on the school trip to Paris, standing in his felt slippers and Paisley dressing gown in the rain outside their hotel watching him hand Clarinda Bain out of a taxi, and his spirit fell even lower. Rachel was right when she told him he could be such a fool.

'I'll take my own car if you don't mind,' he said.

But they did mind. They preferred him to come in theirs.

'So that I won't do a bunk?'

They smiled noncommittally.

They escorted him down his garden path, one going out in front, the other bringing up the rear. He felt as if he were being frog-marched. A dangerous criminal, a

70

sex maniac, who might leap out of the bushes at any young girl who happened to be passing. He did not dare look to right or left for fear of encountering a neighbouring eye. The presence of the well-marked police car in the street would not have gone unnoticed.

After he'd made his statement he half expected to be charged but they said he might go. They would be continuing their investigations, interviewing witnesses, before deciding if there was a case to answer. There would be a case, he didn't doubt that. The Bains, mother and daughter, would stretch their considerable imaginations to the limit. They wanted his blood. How was it that he used to extol the imagination at every opportunity? *Use your imagination!* he would tell his classes. *Don't just sit there like turnip heads*! Some of them had listened.

He went for a walk in the Botanic Garden. He badly needed air and room to breathe. There was space here in this quiet oasis with its wide views of the city skyline. At this time of the morning few people were about except for the occasional mother with a push-chair. The day was fresh but mild and the colours were just beginning to take on the first tinges of autumn. A swirl of wind ruffled the dry leaves sending a bright scatter across the grass in front of him. For a moment, his mind, like his sight, was taken by the colourful pattern of the leaves on the green sward, then it was swamped again by the knowledge that was cutting into the very centre of his being: he was a man under suspicion and, if found guilty, might go to prison, as a sex offender. He stumbled into the rock garden. The gentians were blooming vividly. Flowers that he loved for their intensity of colour. But he had to turn away. The very intensity of that deep blue was making his eyes water. God damn her! Everything he saw or did brought him back to her, and to Paris.

# Chapter Four

They set off on their Rodin pilgrimage on the first morning of their stay in Paris. It was Robbie who dubbed it a pilgrimage.

Clarinda, they were soon to find, had an additional agenda. 'Can we go first to the rue du Cherche-Midi?' she asked. She had her own map and a notebook in which she had written down the various places in Paris she wanted to see, most of them having come from books lent to her by Cormac.

'The rue du Cherche-Midi?' he repeated, then nodded, following the tracking of her mind. He was quite willing to indulge her whim, if it could be so described. He always found enthusiasm difficult to resist and hers was palpable, almost mesmeric.

'Gwen John lived there,' Clarinda explained to the others.

'Gwen John,' echoed Cathy, one of the girls.

'Don't tell me you don't know Gwen John!' reproved Robbie, 'Tut, tut. Such ignorance.'

'Gwen John was a painter, a wonderful painter, sister of Augustus, but better in my opinion,' declared Clarinda, leading the way, map in hand, leaving the rest of the group to straggle untidily behind. 'She's been compared to Modigliani, hasn't she, Cormac?'

'I believe so. Her work is very quiet,' he told the others. 'Very intense and delicate.'

'What's this Gwen woman got to do with it?' grumbled Sue, friend of Cathy. 'I thought it was Rodin we were meant to be after.'

'Apart from being a painter,' said Clarinda over her shoulder, 'she was a model of Rodin's.'

'There's no holding our Clarrie once she gets going,' said Robbie, lengthening his stride to catch up with her.

Their hotel was not far from the rue du Cherche-Midi. They reached it in a few steps.

'Number 87,' said Clarinda. 'Top floor.'

They gazed up at the top of the fourth floor typical Parisian apartment building of the nineteenth century with its long windows and narrow wrought-iron balconies.

'What's that supposed to do for you?' asked Sue.

'I like to see where people lived,' returned Clarinda, 'so that I can imagine them coming along the street, climbing the stairs to their room. It was in that room up there that she painted a number of her most famous paintings.' From her notebook she produced a postcard depicting a basket chair and simple table on which rests a small bowl of flowers, the scene lit by filtered light coming through the muslin-curtained window.

'I can see what you mean by quiet,' said Cathy. 'Not much going on in a room like that.'

'That's all you know,' said Clarinda with a small smile.

Cathy made a face behind Clarinda's back.

'Let's move on,' said Cormac.

'Can we go next to the rue de l'Université?' asked

Clarinda. 'Please! I want to see where Rodin had his atelier.' Cormac had never thought to seek it out himself on previous visits to Paris. He had spent most of his time in the Rodin Museum itself.

'Rodin had his studio in the rue de l'Université before moving to the Hôtel Biron,' Clarinda informed Alec McCaffy, the other teacher accompanying the pupils. '87. Just like Gwen John in the rue du Cherche-Midi. Lucky number.'

Alec was impressed. 'They seem to know their stuff,' he observed to Cormac. He was pleased to see so many of them armed with maps and appeared to think it was due to his influence since he taught geography. He was happy to freely confess to knowing nothing about art, apart from the fact that he had heard of and seen photographs of the Mona Lisa and a few other similarly famous pictures such as Renoir's lusciously appointed ladies or Degas' ballet dancers. His mother had one of the ballet dancers on the lid of a box that had originally contained chocolates but in which she now kept loose buttons. Cormac's mother had also had a button box when he was a child, probably still did. It was something he had in common with Alec McCaffy. He doubted if he had much else.

'Clarinda knows it, anyway,' said Cormac, although he suspected quite a lot had rubbed off on the others too,. He would not expect them to express their enthusiasm so openly, however, since they worked hard to appear laid back.

When they passed number 83 in the rue de l'Universite Cormac began to have doubts. The next building was a corner cafe, and then they were on the Place du Palais Bourbon.

'It's not the kind of area you'd find a studio, Clarinda. It was in the old marble depot if I recall rightly. That's the National Assembly over there. The seat of the government.'

'It said 87 in the book.' Clarinda was frowning.

You can't believe everything you read in books,' said Robbie, skipping over a puddle.

There were several police vans parked on the rim of the square and a considerable number of police gathered in and around it. Some wore protective coverings on their lower limbs and carried riot shields.

'They must be expecting a riot,' said Robbie hopefully. A couple of the policemen had turned to look them over. 'Maybe they'll think we've come to make a protest about student rights. They might even spray us with tear gas. *Bonjour*!' He gave the two policemen a short bow.

'That's enough, Robbie,' said Cormac. Robbie was known at school to be a tempter of providence as well as an occasional truant player. He truanted only when he got bored, so he claimed. He survived because he could do quite brilliant work when he put his mind to it.

It's a pity we don't have a camcorder with us,' said Robbie. 'We could make a video called *Looking for Rodin's ateliér in the rue de l'Université sur la rive gauche de Paris while the police play silly buggers with their riot shields.*'

'And enter it for the Turner Prize,' said Clarinda.

Robbie grinned at her and raised his thumb.

Clarinda was still looking round, hoping for enlightenment. Suddenly she stepped out and stopped a smartly dressed woman woman walking with a small yappy dog on a short lead. '*Excusez-moi, madame. Nous cherchons l'atelier de Rodin.*'

'*Ah, l'atelier de Rodin!*' The woman tapped the dog on its nose to quieten it, then told them that the street numbers had been changed at some point. It seemed to happen in Paris. She shrugged. '*Mais l'atelier de Rodin -*' Why, she believed it had been demolished many years ago.

'Another dream shattered,' sighed Robbie, when woman and dog had departed. 'So much for lucky 87!'

'Oh, shut up, Robbie!' said Clarinda, surprising him and Cormac by her vehemence.

A few days before they were due to leave, Anita Gibb, a member of the English department, came to see him with a couple of sheets of paper in her hand. 'I've got rather an interesting essay here, from one of the fifth years. I thought you might like to read it. It falls into your province, rather.' A little bemused smile was making her bottom lip twitch. 'I set them an essay, you know the kind of thing, a day in the life of. The kind of essay they might have done in primary but I thought it might be interesting to see what they would do with it now. They could choose to do anyone they wished, known or unknown.'

It is spring but the morning is cool, with a chill wind coming off the river. I shiver and pull my coat tightly round me. I am feeling the cold even more than usual because I am nervous about this visit. Of course I am! What woman would not be, going to keep an appointment with a genius? Will he want to model me once he sees me naked? I am conscious of how thin I am where-

77

as I know that he likes his models to be firm-fleshed and mature, with generous breasts and buttocks. My Finnish friend Hilda Flodin, who is a sculptor herself and who introduced me to Rodin, told me that he thinks that young girls are poor specimens in comparison. But he did ask me to come and show him my body so why would he do that unless there was something about me that he found attractive? And I need to earn money. I can't expect to live from my painting.

I knock and wait and while I wait I think about running away. And then the door opens and one of his assistants admits me and conducts me into the high, vaulted room where he works. My eyes are dazzled by the array of female sculptures in every imaginable pose, some of them quite suggestive and daring. They seem almost to be alive. Flodin told me that Paul Claudel, the writer and brother of his former mistress, Camille, called them a 'banquet of buttocks'. I hesitate in front of such a formidable array. I want to turn and run again, for I know I cannot ever expect to measure up to women like these, but he is coming towards me, the great man himself, in his long white smock, with his strong head and bushy white beard, his hands held out to mine, and my heart is leaping. I take his hands, I could not refuse, and he leads me kindly to the stove, and brings forward a wicker chair and sits me down. I want to faint.

'Warm yourself,' he says. 'There's no hurry.'

I feel overwhelmed by him, this giant of a man. He puts me at my ease, he is gentle, so when it is time for me to go to the model's couch behind the screens and take off my clothes my nervousness has gone. I even feel proud of my body. I stand erect and await his verdict.

He tells me that I have '*un corps admirable*.' I glow with pleasure, I am no longer cold. He says he likes my legs and my swan-like neck. I lift my head high.

'Come tomorrow,' he says.

From that moment onward I know that I shall be prepared to come whenever he wishes and to do whatever he wishes. I am entranced by him. I am happy with my nudity and I know that I shall be happy to be with him. When the work is finished for the day and the assistants leave he will light candles in wine bottles and then we shall be alone together. We shall kiss in the warm, flickering light, and that will be the beginning of something wonderful. I can feel his hands on my body, moving over it, caressing it. I will cry out. Each time we are left alone he will make love to me. It will be the moment of the day that I wait for, hunger for. I will never have enough of him. I do not care that he is sixty-three years old and I am so much younger, and that he might tire when making love more quickly than me. Flodin says he claims that sex makes him feel old but I cannot believe that. I know it will it make me feel young and liberated.

Cormac, remembering the essay now, looked at Clarinda frowning with frustration over her map. 'I don't think there's any point in looking any further,' he said.

'Since we have obviously been chasing wild geese,' said Robbie.

Clarinda came reluctantly. They turned back along the rue de l'Université and headed up past the massive pile of Invalides to the rue de Varenne and the Rodin Museum, formerly the Hôtel Biron, where Rodin had installed himself in 1908, renting the room on the ground floor with three tall windows looking onto the garden.

'Gwen hated it when he left his old studio,' said Clarinda. 'She found the old one more friendly.'

'Familiar, aren't we?' said Robbie. '*Gwen.*'

'What do you mean by friendly?' asked Cathy.

'Intimate?' suggested Robbie.

Clarinda was not to be drawn.

Before going into the house she went purposefully round the garden until she found the black marble statue she was seeking. The rest followed, as if she, with the long pale hair streaming behind her, were the Pied Piper. *The Muse*, sculpted as a memorial to Whistler, stood above them, armless, head bowed, mouth slightly open, her right foot lifted onto a high rock. Rodin had intended to do the arms at some point but had never got round to it. Cormac explained that Rodin often put together limbs and bits and pieces of bodies afterwards. In the museum out at Meudon one could see rows of casts for arms and legs and hands.

'Gwen John was the model,' said Clarinda, her eyes fixed on the downturned face.

'Camille Claudel was his most important model,' put in Cormac. It seemed necessary to get things into perspective.

'Didn't she go off her head?' said Robbie. 'Camille? Maybe all his models did.'

'The statues she posed for are the most erotic and sensuous,' said Cormac.

It was so much easier here in Paris to speak of sensuality and eroticism than back in Edinburgh within the constraints of the classroom where the pupils tended to giggle or catcall. Here they were determined to show they were fully fledged adults. Most of them had probably had some sexual experience, if statistics were to be believed, and in this instance he was sure that they were. He had read somewhere that the average starting age for having sex in the UK was 15.3 years, whereas globally it was 15.9. These young people were not as he had been at sixteen and seventeen, gauche in his encounters with the opposite sex, and, apart from any experiences they had had themselves, they went regularly to the cinema and saw films marked 18.

'If you look at Gwen's face here or in her self-portrait,' said Clarinda, 'you would never imagine that she was so sensual and so passionate. Or so wild.'

'I suppose she had it off with Rodin too, like all the others?' said Robbie.

Clarinda ignored him and continued to address Cormac. 'She seems so demure, wouldn't you say? Do you remember reading about how she sat on rocks at the edge of the sea on the Welsh coast and a huge wave came and swept her out to sea and then swept her back in again? She called it "delicious danger".' Clarinda lingered over the last two words. 'I understand that.'

'You do?' He did remember something about Gwen John liking to swim naked and go far out to sea but did not recall her being swept off rocks. But then it was a long time since he had read about her life, and indeed had not given it much thought until now. 'It can sometimes be a mistake to get too interested in the lives of artists,' he cautioned. 'Especially taking one particular aspect of them, for that can distort the person.' Rachel had once accused him of caricaturing his aunts by dwelling on their oddities whereas much of the time they were douce women living quietly and minding their own business; he had responded that it was their peculiarities that made them interesting and brought them into relief. But aunts did not come into the same category as artists whom one did not know in a personal way. 'Better to concentrate on the work, Clarinda' he went on. 'That, after all, is what matters.'

'But when Gwen was unhappy it affected her work! She had no energy, she couldn't paint. If you were unhappy could you go on with your work?'

'It could be a diversion from unhappiness.' He was to find that this would not be so in his case.

The exhibits in both the garden and the building inspired all them, even those like Cathy and Sue who had probably come on the trip for the city of Paris itself more than its art. The students wandered around entranced by the sheer beauty of the sculptures, their energy and charged emotion. They circled round the larger pieces, such as *The Burghers of Calais*, in wonder, eager to see them fully and from all angles, going back to them again and again. They squatted on the floor inside the high, spacious rooms and on the grass outside drawing busily in their sketch books. They kept remarking how alive the pieces seemed, as Cormac had told them that they would. He was pleased, of course he was, and their responses made him reflect how fortunate he was to be a teacher with the opportunity to inspire young minds. That was what he thought at that moment as he stood by one of the long windows looking out into the garden, as Rodin himself must often have done.

It was *The Kiss*, predictably, the man and woman

locked together in perpetuity, their marble-white bodies fluid and graceful, flowing the one into the other, dependent on each other, that held the students especially enthralled, but Clarinda in particular. She studied it for a long time.

Even Alec was impressed. 'He certainly had something, that guy.'

They could have an hour, Cormac told the group, to wander round on their own. 'Take your time, look, sketch, photograph, but don't leave the grounds, and meet in the garden outside the front door afterwards. Understood?'

He knew some of them would make for the cafe in the garden but he did not mind. They had all had a pretty good look already. As he moved on his own from room to room and along the garden paths enjoying the bright sunshine he observed some of them, still looking, still sketching. He saw Robbie intently sketching *The Thinker* but saw no sign of Clarinda.

When they gathered after the hour was up she was missing.

'Anyone seen Clarinda?' asked Cormac, scanning the garden.

Nobody had.

'Maybe she's run off with Rodin's ghost,' said Robbie, which raised a laugh. 'Or Gwen's? That might be even more interesting.'

Cormac asked him to nip round the back and see if Clarinda might be taking a last look at *The Muse*. He returned saying, 'Not a sign. She's vanished! There's a lot of that thin air hanging about.'

Five minutes later Clarinda came rushing out of the building. 'Sorry.' She was slightly breathless . 'I forgot the time.'

'Where have you been?' asked Cormac.

'In the archives. I asked and they were terribly nice. I hope that was all right?'

She didn't have to tell him what she would have been doing there. What exactly was going on in this girl's mind? How could he possibly guess? He did not know what went on in his daughter's head much of the time and he had watched over her since birth.

'What's up, Dad?' asks Sophie, laying her warm hand on top of his cold one. 'Are you feeling all right?'

'Yes, fine,' he mutters, turning his back on Clarinda who is sitting at a corner table of the bistro talking animatedly to a young man. She has noticed him, he knows that; he saw the rapid flicker of her eyelids, although she did not look in his direction. And she was talking and gesticulating too wildly, which is unlike her. The display was for his benefit, he suspects.

He regards his daughter, who goes to a different school than the one where he taught, which is fortunate. They had to tell her about Clarinda, of course; it would have been impossible not to. When they did she blushed and looked startled at the idea of her father being embroiled in such an affair but said nothing for a moment. Then she asked aggressively, without looking at him, 'Are you innocent or guilty?' Rachel was outraged, too much so, in his opinion, for it seemed a legitimate question to ask. Perhaps it was one that Rachel herself would have liked to ask outright instead of pussyfooting around it, as she had been doing. 'How can you even doubt your father, Sophie!' her mother demanded. 'He needs all the support we can give him.'

Sophie clicks her fingers at a waitress and calls out, 'Two more glasses of red wine, please!'

'Sophie!' he protests weakly. He feels weak and at the same time angry that Clarinda Bain should have such an effect on him. He wants to put his hands round her smooth young neck and throttle her.

'I can drink far more than that,' says Sophie. 'I won't fall over in the gutter or anything like that.'

He doesn't doubt it. 'How much do you drink anyway? Too much?'

'Not regularly.'

'You're not into drugs, are you? You wouldn't, would you?'

'No, I wouldn't. Not real drugs. I've had the odd smoke but that's all, honest!'

The wine comes and they drink it and he doesn't allow himself to turn his head, though his ear is cocked, listening for sounds coming from the table behind him. He hears the rise and fall of Clarinda's voice and then, later, the scrape of chairs which suggests they are preparing to leave. He keeps his eyes down and remembers Rodin's statue of *The Muse* with downcast eyes and Clarinda studying it, enraptured. A shadow falls over the table and passes on. It was her; he recognised her walk. Then comes a second shadow and a voice says, 'Cormac, how're you doing?'

He looks up at Robbie.

'Not bad.' He introduces Sophie. 'How're you doing yourself, Robbie?'

'I'm at the uni. Doing architecture.'

'Great! Nice to see you.'

'You too.'

Robbie leaves to join Clarinda.

'Shall we get the bill?' says Cormac.

When it arrives he takes out his wallet. He looks inside. He leans on one hip and rummages in his trouser pocket.

'What's the matter?' asks Sophie. 'Haven't you got enough money?'

'Not quite. It was the extra wine. And I've forgotten my damned cheque book. Damn and blast!'

'How much are you short?'

'Four forty. Got anything on you?.'

'Hang on.' From the depths of her drawstring bag Sophie produces a purse shaped like a pouch that is also drawn together round the neck by a cord. The purse is bulging with coins. They come spilling out when she loosens the string. He catches two fifty pence pieces before they bounce off the table onto the floor. Sophie lays out in small heaps on the table four pounds forty pence in two, five, ten and twenty pence pieces. When she has finished the purse is still more than half full. How has she come to have so many coins? Has she been *busking*? But she can't sing, as far as he's aware, and the only instrument she plays is a piano, which is not suited to being dragged onto the streets. He doesn't ask the question. *Typical of you, Cormac!* He can hear Rachel's voice in his ear. She would certainly ask.

When she rings that evening she has plenty of questions to put to him. 'Did you ask Sophie?' is only the beginning.

'Ask her what?'

'What she does when she plays hookey. Cormac, don't tell me you forgot!'

'I didn't get round to it, but I will. We were talking about other things.'

'You're hopeless.'

'Thank you.'

'Where is she now?'

'Out.'

'Out where?'

'She didn't tell me. You know what fifteen-year-old girls are like.'

'Did you ask?'

'Well, no.'

'I always ask.'

'And do you think she always tell you the truth? I believe she was going out with her friend Tilda.'

'Tilda,' sniffs Rachel. 'Mm.'

'How's Davy?' he asks.

'Fine. He's in bed, fast asleep. He was very tired.'

He senses an accusation in that statement: Davy is catching up on his sleep because he has not had enough during the week when he was with his father. In truth, Davy has had a number of late nights recently. Cormac becomes restless when he is forced to spend evening after evening cooped up in the small space of the Colony flat. They have gone out to eat a few times, usually to Henderson's, a vegetarian restaurant, an Edinburgh institution, and sat listening to men playing guitars and banjos. He'll have to put a stop to it, this eating out. No wonder he didn't have enough money to pay the bill at lunchtime. Remembering that and the coins pouring out of Sophie's purse he feels uneasy.

'How much pocket money are you giving Sophie?' he asks.

Rachel tells him. 'Why do you ask?'

'Nothing. No reason.' He shouldn't have asked. Rachel could catch any nuance floating on the wind; her antennae are permanently on alert.

'I must go,' she says. 'Catch up on the ironing.' She claims to find ironing a soothing occupation, once you surrender and get down to it. He seldom manages to get down to it but vows that he must try and send out Davy to school looking a bit smoother.

When he replaces the receiver he realises that it is Saturday evening and he may do as he chooses since he is free from child-care. Ken Mason, a former colleague, has invited him to a party. He hasn't been in a mind to go until now when he sees the empty evening yawning ahead. Ken is the only one of the staff to have kept in touch with him. After his suspension Cormac found the others, when he did run into them, backed away quickly, looking at their watches, remembering imminent appointments. The neighbours also gave him a wide berth. There was a report in the *Scotsman* that did not name him initially but he imagined that everyone in Edinburgh must know that it was him. He felt like a marked man, and at the slightest blink of sun he took to wearing dark glasses.

'Claims that an Edinburgh art teacher made sexual advances to a female pupil during a recent trip to Paris are being investigated by Edinburgh and Lothian police. After twenty pupils and two teachers returned from France the police were contacted by the girl's mother, who claimed that the behaviour of the teacher in question towards her daughter had been inappropriate. A spokeswoman said that enquiries were still at an early stage and all the pupils who had been on the trip would be questioned. It is understood that the girl, at the time, was fifteen.'

# Chapter Five

He decides to go to Ken Mason's party rather than sit in the flat feeling sorry for himself. The Masons live on the other side of town, the south side. He puts on his cycling cape and bumps his bike down the steps. It is fair when he sets out but half way there the sleet starts and by the time he reaches his destination his slicker is dripping and his legs are sodden from the knee down. He throws off the slicker and eases his cords away from his knees. He probably shouldn't have worn cords, come to think of it; he always relied on Rachel to tell him what to wear when they were going out, she seems to have a sixth sense that tells her these things. Through the lit-up, uncurtained bay window he sees a room full of dark suits. He only has one suit, bought at an Oxfam shop, which he keeps for weddings and funerals. Funerals, mostly. That reminds him: he must ring his mother tomorrow. It's her birthday. Her eighty-first.

Lorna Mason opens the door to him. A heavy wave of perfume gushes out from her.

'I've got wet knees, I'm afraid.'

'Sounds sexy.' He doesn't like her smile.

'Doesn't feel it, I'm afraid. My cords are clinging to me.'

'Perhaps we could find you a pair of Ken's trousers. What size would you be?' She gazes at his lower half.

He backs away. 'No, no, these'll soon dry.'

'Trust you to come on your bike on a filthy night like this, Cormac. You artists! So impractical. Do you want to bring it in?' She is looking dubiously at the bike.

'I'll just padlock it to the railings, if your neighbours wouldn't object?'

Lorna takes his slicker between her raspberry-tipped fingernails and hurries it at arm's length through to the rear premises before it can make too many drips on her parquet hall floor. Cormac follows on, uttering cries of apology for being such a nuisance.

'It's all right, Cormac, I don't mind. It's so lovely to see you. It's been ages.' She plants a raspberry kiss on his cheek, then leans back to study his face. 'You have been having an awful time of it, haven't you, poor you? Girls these days are such hussies. One of my mother's words.' She laughs. 'So forward, aren't they? In my day we wouldn't have *dreamt* of looking at a teacher. Well, we might just have looked, but we certainly wouldn't have *touched.* I'm always warning Ken to beware, to keep a clear space between him and the pupils, and what happened to you just proves it.'

She takes him through to the sitting room, puts a drink into his hand and introduces him to a woman whose name he doesn't catch. She is around his own age and he notices that she is not wearing a wedding ring. He has started to notice such things, whereas before they would never register. 'You're a bachelor now,' Ken told him on the phone. 'Free, in the market again, up for grabs.' Ken sounded envious. After Cormac was charged they had a few drinks together and Ken said, 'I've always thought she was a bit of all right, Miss Clarinda Bain,' and he moved in closer to Cormac at the bar expecting a confidence. 'She's got fantastic legs. And boobs. Her mother's not bad, either. Think she rather fancies me, does Mrs Bain. She gave me the eye at the last Parents' Night.'

The woman he has been introduced to reveals that she is an insurance broker. 'You're a colleague of Ken's, I believe?'

'Was. I've changed careers.'

'How interesting. I admire people with the courage to do that. What are you doing now? Did you have to re-train?"

He tells her that he is a sandwich-maker and she smiles, somewhat wanly, not knowing whether he is having her on or not, and he sympathises. Making small talk at parties is bloody awful and the reason that he usually avoids them. If he were to say so now that might relax them both but he can't be bothered and he doesn't want to encourage her, or anybody else. For that was his downfall, after all, wasn't it? Giving encouragement, without sufficient thought. It was irresponsible, leading your students into the world of the imagination. Anyway, he doesn't like the woman's lower lip; it's too thin and bloodless. You're too fussy, Ken would say. It's not long before the woman sees someone across the room that she ought to speak to and excuses herself.

He finishes his drink and seeks out another. Once he has a goodly amount of alcohol in him he finds the party tolerable and chats idly to a number of people whom he will not remember the next day and is happy not to. It is a way of passing time. He makes a move to leave before the main decampment. Lorna, who has been guzzling gin, sees him unsteadily to the door.

'Why don't you drop in and see me sometime, Cormac? You're always out and about on your bicycle, aren't you? I'd invite you to lunch but you can't do lunch, can you? You have those frightful sandwiches to make. What a bore. But what about after lunch? A post-prandial drink? It's nice and quiet here at that time of day. You can't have to look after Davy every afternoon surely? He must go to swimming or karate or something. All the kids do. I'll phone you.'

He plants a swift kiss on her proffered face, since it is expected, managing to avoid her mouth, less raspberry-coloured than it was earlier but still not appealing, then he hoists himself back into the saddle and takes off. It feels good to have the road running underneath him again. He doesn't even mind the sleet-laden wind in his face.

The city looks magical under its soft falling curtain of white, the lights from the lamps fuzzy and blurred, the greyness of the stone muted, the sound of traffic dimmed. At the top of the Mound he slows to look down at the spread of lights in Princes Street below. A passing car comes too close and the bike wobbles in its back draught; he curses and tries to right the machine but the road is slippery and he goes into a skid and in the next instant he hits the road and the back wheel is spinning in the air.

He was eight years old, the age his son is now. He was coming too fast down the hill, as he was often tempted to do, and had many times done, but this time he was not going to be able to stop, he knew he was not, the road was glassy after a drizzle of rain, and he had left braking too late. Another child on a bicycle pulled out of a side street, straight into his path. He swerved, squeezing both brakes hard, and was thrown up and over over the handlebars to hit the road. The rest was blackness, until some hours later he awoke in a swoon of whiteness to find his mother by his bed, flanked by two of the aunts, Lily and Sal. The faces of the women looked wretched and pale. His mother reached for his hand.

'Cormac, thanks be to God. We've been praying for you throughout the night and the Lord has seen fit to answer our prayers. Can you hear me, son?'

Yes, he could hear her though her voice seemed distant and disembodied, as if it were coming from somewhere in the air above her. Sal gave him a drink of water, holding the tumbler to his mouth. His teeth clunked against the glass, water dribbled down his cheek. He ran his tongue along the rim of his lips; they felt scored, like sandpaper. Suddenly, he remembered the greasy road and that terrible feeling of losing control and the boy coming out of the side road.

He found his voice.

'What happened to the other boy?' he cried.

'Now don't go fussing yourself, son,' said Lily, tucking the sheet in tidily around him. All of the aunts called him son so that often he felt he had five mothers, all of whom but Sal took it upon themselves to watch over his moral wellbeing. Sal was the subversive one in the family and had already been married and divorced.

'Is he all right?' Cormac struggled to sit up.

'Hush now, love,' said his mother. 'Lie back there and rest yourself. It wasn't your fault. It was an accident.'

He was allowed to go home after a week in hospital but it took him many more weeks to recover fully. He had a broken leg and arm and he suffered from headaches. Every night he dreamt of the boy emerging from the side street and he wakened screaming.

'It was my fault,' he told his mother.

'Nonsense,' she said, holding him so close that he could feel her heart beating. 'It was an accident. A man and a woman waiting on a bus saw it all happening. They say the boy came out without looking. They told the police.'

'But if I'd braked earlier -'

'You mustn't blame yourself, son. Nobody else does.'

What about God? He was all-seeing, all-knowing. He must have seen him coming down the hill too fast. Cormac tried to confess but the priest blocked his confession, telling him, as his mother had, that it was an accident and no blame was attributed to him.

'You don't have to go around feeling guilty, lad. You didn't want to kill that boy, did you?'

Of course he hadn't. He hadn't even known him and was glad of that, at least. He could no longer bear to go down the street where the boy had lived, in case he'd see the boy's mother's face at the window. There were a lot of things he couldn't bear. Some were understandable, the adults agreed, like the sight of a bicycle. But school now, that was a different matter. When it was time for him to go back he started to vomit. His mother was worried sick.

'Leave him be for a while, Mrs Aherne,' advised the doctor. 'Let him do his school work at home. He'll come back to his old self, given time.'

His aunts brought him books and games to play like

Ludo and Monopoly. He liked it best when Sal came. She was the youngest of the sisters, his mother the eldest. Sal smoked flat Turkish cigarettes in a jade green holder and said things that made him laugh. She talked to him about the man she'd married. His name was Jake. Jake the rake, she called him. He had run off with another woman, which didn't seem to have bothered her. 'It was good riddance. I married him too hastily. He had a soft tongue on him, heavy on the charm, you know what I mean? He could talk you into anything, but he was light on the follow up. I'm doing rightly on my own.' She had a job as a saleswoman in the lingerie department of Anderson and McAuleys. Ten years further down the line she would annoy her family further by up and marrying a Dublin publican whose pub she inherited on his early death. The life suited her.

One day, she arrived carrying a large box.

'Clay,' she announced, setting it on the table. 'For making models. Then you can fire them in the oven. I remember when you were small how you were always making things with plasticene. You've got good strong square hands, like your da had. Your hands remind me of his. You remind me a lot of him though I wouldn't say that if your mother was around.' His mother had gone to do her turn at cleaning the church.

That was the beginning for him. The clay absorbed him. His fingers began to work, to knead, to mould, and, finally, a shape would begin to emerge, the reward, bringing with it a rush of pleasure. 'Look, Mum!' he'd cry. 'That's not bad, son,' she'd say, nodding her head. He made the animals that went into the ark, two by two, and then he made Noah and Noah's wife. His mother approved of the biblical theme. She baked his creations, as she called them, in the oven and didn't even complain about the cost of the gas. He began, too, to build shapes from other materials, spent matchsticks, empty packets, sewing spools stripped of their thread, kirby grips and hat pins. His mother said she could leave nothing lying about. It was like having a magpie in the house. But she smiled while she said it.

'He loves making things so he does,' his mother said to Sal. 'He's at it all day long. It'll be a nice hobby for him so it will.'

Shortly afterwards, Sal persuaded him to get back on his bike.

Coming up the steps, carrying his bike on his shoulder, he hears his phone ringing and wonders who it could be at this hour of the night. Rachel always says that when the phone rings late it's usually someone from Ireland. The Irish on the whole go to bed later than the Scots and think nothing of phoning for a midnight chat. His mother! She wouldn't phone herself, she is an early bedder, but it could be one of her sisters or a neighbour to say she's had a fall and can he come over. He awaits that news which some day surely must come. As he fumbles with the key he wonders why Sophie doesn't answer the damned thing. He told her to be back by twelve and it's now gone one. She could be sleeping the sleep of the dead, she's capable of it. The ringing is going on and on. He pushes open the door, drops the bike and hurries into the living room.

The caller is Sal.

'Sal,' he says with relief. 'Thank God!'

She laughs. She has just closed her tavern and feels

like a chat. He can see her sitting in the rosy glow of her upstairs' flat dressed in a satin blouse with long, tight-fitting puffed sleeves, a pearl choker round her plump neck, pearl earrings dangling, spinning in the light, her hair swept up on top, Edwardian-style. She always dresses up to go behind the bar, likes her customers to feel that a night out in Sal's place is something special. She claims to have the best fiddlers in town playing for her. She'll have a dram beside the telephone on the Chinese lacquered table and a cheroot smouldering between her fingers.

'Wish I were there with you, Sal.'

'Wish you were, too, son. Why don't you come over? Give up that sandwich bar your mother's been telling me about and come and help me in a real bar. I'm proposing cutting you in on the business, Cormac. I won't be here for ever, no, don't bother telling me I'm immortal. Who'd want that? When I need a zimmer I'll be off. I'm leaving you the pub in my will. Who else would I leave it to? You're the only heir for the lot of us, think of that! So why not come over and get stuck in before I tootle off? I'm not planning to go for a good while yet. I'm not long past seventy, for dear sake. We could have good crack together, Cormac.'

He is tempted, oh yes, he is. A new start, away from the gossip and the possibility of the running into Clarinda Bain, away from Rachel's orbit and the constant reminder of her. But there are the kids to consider. Whatever way he turns he can't get away from them, doesn't want to get away from them. It is easy enough for Sal to say bring the wee lad with you, he'd soon settle into Dublin, but Rachel would never agree.

Talk of the children reminds him that Sophie is in his

97

charge until tomorrow, or rather, later today. He says, 'Hang on a sec, Sal, I've just got to check something.'

He limps up the stairs, registering the pain in his left foot where it was crushed under the bike and pushes open the door of Davy's room where Sophie is to sleep for the night. Should even now be sleeping. His premonition was right; the bed is flat and the room has that air of stillness when no one has disturbed it for some time. Swearing, he retraces his steps back down the stairs, placing his injured foot carefully. As he goes to lift the receiver he sees a note lying on the table.

'Gone to a party with Tilda at Mandy's, staying the night. Thought you wouldn't want me to walk home on my own late. See you tomorrow. Sophie x.'

Who the hell is Mandy and where does she live? The name doesn't ring a bell. Rachel would know, would probably have Mandy's phone number in her little book. She has always insisted on having the phone numbers of Sophie's friends when she goes to stay with them overnight. What time is it? Getting on for two. Too late to phone Rachel. He chats to Sal for another few minutes but when he goes to bed he's restless and keeps waking up and looking at his watch. He imagines his daughter at a rave in some dark cavern, popping Ecstasy tablets, collapsing unconscious on the floor. In the next sequence she is walking down a dark, empty street, and a man is waiting in the shadows, poised on the balls of his feet, ready to pounce. Now she is crossing the road, and a crazy drunken driver is swerving, coming straight at her. This is ridiculous! More than that, it is ludicrous, and in the morning, in its sober light, he will know and acknowledge that. He is working himself up into a lather when she is probably fast asleep in a bed at Mandy's house with Mandy's mother and father in the next room. He cannot quite talk himself into believing that! So what *would* she doing at this time of night? He knows she is most likely to be in the arms of a member of the opposite sex.

He goes out early in the morning to buy a paper, hoping he might catch sight of his daughter legging it homeward. There aren't many people about and they are mostly people like himself carrying newspapers. There is no sign of a girl in a long woollen coat with a twirl of coloured scarves thrown across her throat.

'Sophie, I could murder you,' he mutters and a woman, dressed in a churchy hat, looks round at him.

He goes into a cafe and orders coffee and a croissant.

In a cafe on the Boulevard St Germain, they ordered coffee and croissants. They needed a rest; their feet were weary after so much pavement-pounding. Cormac was making them walk everywhere rather than resort to travelling underground on the Metro. It was the only way to see the city, he insisted. Never mind a few blisters. Keep your eyes open.

They seemed to have mislaid the others, on the way back from the Musée D'Orsay. They had been talking and not noticed that they had gone so far out in front.

'I like the Impressionists,' said Clarinda defiantly. Some of the group predictably had been calling them old hat. Cormac despaired at times of their reactions; they were so predictable. 'Surprise me!' he often told them.

'Most eras in art have something worth looking at. It's a mistake to be too dismissive. You miss too much. The main thing is that it should give you pleasure.'

'Oh, it does!' said Clarinda with ardour.

In the morning, they had gone to the Orangerie to see Monet's water lilies. They'd gone early so that they were there when the museum opened and they'd had the place to themselves for the first quarter of an hour and been able to see the walls unimpeded. The water lilies had scored a hundred per cent with the pupils. Tomorrow they would go to Giverny to see Monet's garden.

'I'm dying to see it!' said Clarinda.

It was so agreeable to sit at a Parisian pavement cafe, with all the echoes that that evoked, and talk about painting. The vision it conjured up seemed almost to be a cliché, he observed to Clarinda, but she did not comprehend. Clichés came from over-use. She had not lived long enough yet. She enjoyed each thing for what it was, which was one of the things that he had learned about her on this trip and, of course, liked. Her reactions were fresh.

'I love pavement cafes,' she cried gaily. 'I love Paris!'

'It's easy to love it,' he agreed. Their table was sitting in a pool of sunlight.

'I can understand Gwen John wanting to live and work here, even though she did have a difficult time with money and had to pose for other artists. She didn't mind posing for Rodin though, she said she loved that. He must have been a very charismatic man.'

'What did you make of her letters?'

Clarinda was not ready to answer straight away, she needed to take time to consider.

'Do you think Rodin made her happy?' prompted Cormac.

'At times. But not all the time. My mother says you

100

can't expect someone to make you happy *all* the time but if they make you happy some of the time then that's a bonus. Gwen wasn't happy when she'd swept and cleaned her room and was waiting for Rodin to come and he didn't come. And of course she wrote the letters when she was alone so often they wouldn't have been her best times.'

'She did a lot of waiting, I think?'

'Yes, but sometimes waiting is not all that bad. Not if you're waiting *for* someone.'

'Only if you are sure they will come.'

She nodded. She opened her bag and took out her notebook. 'She refers to him as *Mon Maître* always. Here she says nothing else matters after an embrace from her ... *amant*.' Clarinda's cheeks looked hot. Her head was inclined over the book. 'All her previous disappointments were then effaced. She speaks quite openly about ... things. His hands. Her body. How she felt when they made love. It must have been a grand passion.'

'Or a fantasy?'

'A fantasy?' Clarinda looked up. 'Oh, no, I don't think so. If you read these letters you wouldn't say that. She pours out her heart to him, without shame. And there are so many of them and they went on for a long time. For years.'

'Perhaps it's not possible to know.' He smiled. 'So, do you fancy coming to live in Paris and being an artist?'

"Yes, I do, after I've been to college. I'll rent a room and paint.'

'And starve.'

'Don't be cynical! Don't you have any faith in me? Don't you think I'll be any good?' She removed her dark glasses and he saw that there were sparks in her eyes. She really cared about her work. That was not so very extraordinary. He had cared, too, when he was her age. He had been single-minded.

'I think you could be good,' he answered cautiously. She did have talent though she would need to work at it, like all of them on the trip.

'Didn't you ever dream of coming here to live?'

She had touched a nerve that still had the power to jangle. Of course he'd had his dreams, like every other young person.

'I got married and had children. I had to make a living.'

'That was your choice, then.'

It was easy to see things simply, at her age, he wanted to tell her, but did not, for it would only sound patronising. But her passion made him feel wistful.

'I like your work,' she said. 'I liked your wire sculptures in particular. I liked the humour in them.' He was pleased at her perception. He had had an exhibition in the summer and some of his fifth and sixth year students had visited it. They had been surprised that his work didn't look much like Rodin's.

'Why did you think it would?' he'd asked them.

'You always said he influenced you.'

'That doesn't mean I aped his work. Influences are more subtle than that.'

'I couldn't agree more, Mr Aherne,' Mrs Bain had said. She had come with her daughter. 'I know that myself. I am a great admirer of Burns but I would not presume to think that my poetry in any way resembles his.' Clarinda had half turned her back to hide her discomfiture and was closely examining an exhibit. Her mother had adored everything as soon as she had put a foot over the gallery threshold and wished that she had enough money to buy the lot! 'I would fill my house with your treasures, Mr Aherne, if I could,' she had told him.

He had seldom met a more invasive woman, he reflected, as he sat on a cafe terrace on the Boulevard St Germain remembering Mrs Bain at his exhibition. It was a wonder she had not found a way to accompany them to Paris. He found her quite alarming when she presented herself at his door on parents' evenings, dressed in lurid, floating garments which concealed her size and shape, with jangling bangles encircling her plump wrists and various assorted chains hung about her person, and smelling so strongly of some musty scent that he had to move his head back to avoid suffocation. She talked too close to his face for comfort and he was too conscious of her plummy lips and the traces of lipstick on her teeth. She painted a little herself, she had confided on one visit, dropping her voice to a confidential manner. Watercolours. Oh, she was sure he would think nothing of them. She went to classes, though, and her teacher had been kind enough to say that she could be good enough to be a professional painter with a little more experience. She thought Clarinda must take after her. Apart from Clarinda's own tendency to wear floating Indian cotton dresses he could see nothing of the mother in the daughter. Perhaps she took after the father who had ducked out of their lives many moons ago, possibly driven out of the house by the stench of perfume and the sound of rattling bangles.

'I know he was thirty-five years older than her but

it didn't seem to matter,' said Clarinda. For a moment Cormac was not following. 'Gwen and Rodin,' she went on. 'My mother says age is irrelevant. She says she feels no different from what she did at eighteen.'

'Really?'

'You don't agree?'

'Unfortunately not.'

A waiter had cleared the dirty cups from their table and was hovering, hoping for a fresh order.

'Another cappuccino?' Cormac asked Clarinda and without waiting for an answer he ordered for them both.

'Do you know,' she said, 'I think you could be almost as good as Rodin. I do! If you were to concentrate on your sculpture and give up teaching.'

He laughed. 'Come now, Clarinda! You're just buttering me up. Rodin is a giant. I am scarcely knee-high to him.'

'Why don't you have more faith in yourself?' she demanded fiercely. His laughter faded, and their eyes engaged.

At that moment, the rest of the group burst upon them with cries of 'There you are!' and 'Where have you been?'

When he returns home, having eaten his croissant and drunk two cups of black coffee and read his Sunday newspaper while doing so, he finds the flat still echoingly quiet. No further notes have been left on the table saying, 'Gone to Claire's or Timbuktu.' It is now midday. He is wondering whether to call Rachel and ask her if she knows anyone called Mandy when the phone springs into life, startling him. He grabs the receiver, almost knocking the machine off the table.

'Hi, Dad!' Sophie is phoning from a call box and sounds breathless. She begins to gabble and he wants to break in and say, 'Hey, slow down,' but she isn't listening. 'Listen, Dad,' she says, which is what he's doing, 'I'll be home in a couple of hours, maybe less. OK? Don't worry. No, I'm fine, I tell you. No problems. I haven't got any more change, I'm just about to run out.' The phone goes dead.

He rattles the receiver rest futilely. So she didn't have any more coins. What has happened to all those other coins that she had yesterday? Or has she just been lying? And if she has been lying what else is she covering up? In the meantime he might as well go out and have a pint at the pub.

On his return, the phone is ringing again. It is his Aunt Lily.

'Now listen, son,' she starts. He is tired of people telling him to listen, and calling him son. Last night he dreamt of his two dead aunts, Deirdre and Eithne. They appeared before him dressed in purple stain and rose pink respectively though in his dream he had not been sure which was which. They shimmied their hips. 'Son, son', he heard them keening. He wakened sweating and had to peel off his pyjama jacket. How had he come to be the answerable son to so many women? Seven sisters and only one to bear a child. What a burden to lay upon a child. But he got the message a long time ago: there is no escape, not while any of them are still alive.

Lily's voice is slurred, suggesting her hand has been

in and out of her sewing basket where she keeps her halfs of Bushmills. She hasn't sewn a stitch in years; her sliken embroidery threads have thinned and dulled. She was disappointed in love, so Sal says. Well, who hasn't been? Maybe love is bound to disappoint. God, he's getting cynical in his old age. Old age! How Sal would scoff. You're only forty odd, she would tell him, young enough to begin afresh. He is too anxious right now to feel either fresh or young. He can think only of his daughter. He is half listening to Lily. Although her speech might not be totally clear she is by no means drunk. She enjoys a dram or two, just enough to take the edge off and relax her. 'I know it's none of my business, son,' she says, as if that would make any difference to what she would or would not say, 'but your mother's near up the wall and you know her blood pressure's not good, don't you? She tells me you've lost your job and your wife.'

He could make a smart remark about that being an achievement in itself, the loss of both together, but it would be wasted on his aunt. 'There's nothing I can do about it, Aunt Lily.'

'You could come over and see your mother.' And face the Inquisition.

'Look, I'll need to go, Aunt Lily, I can hear the door. I think it might be Sophie coming in.'

This time, he has told not a word of a lie, for it is his daughter arriving home. She greets him cheerfully, while avoiding his eye. It's cold, isn't it, she says, rubbing her mittened hands together. He takes a long look at her while she is divesting herself of some of the scarves and the long woollen coat. She looks rather grimy to him, as if she hasn't washed that morning or maybe even the night before. And doesn't she pong a bit? He'd better not say that! But aren't those lacy threads clinging to the hem of her coat *cobwebs*?

'Where does this Mandy live then?'

'What do you mean - *this* Mandy?'

'Well, whoever she is.'

'She lives near the Meadows. She's all right, you'd approve of her! Her dad is a lecturer at the university.'

'I don't know that that makes her all right. You could give your dad a kiss when you come in.'

'Sorry.' She comes closer and he kisses her frosted pink cheek. His nose twitches. He was right: her hair smells manky.

'You could be doing with a bath, young lady.'

'I am just going to have one.'

'Mandy not have a bath in her house?'

'I didn't like to use their hot water.'

She's lying. He'd like to grab her by the collar and whirl her round and demand to know the truth, but he doesn't. He says, 'Better get your skates on. We're due at your mother's for lunch.'

They have Sunday lunch as a family. That was part of the agreement, part of the effort to make the children feel that they are a family still, that it has not totally fallen apart.

Cormac carves the corn-fed organic chicken, Rachel spoons out the mashed neeps flavoured with nutmeg and cream and the red cabbage cooked with apples and cloves and the shining, golden-brown roast potatoes. Everything on the table is organic. He has not had such a good meal since the Sunday before. He resolves to do a bit more proper cooking for himself and Davy; they are having too many carry-in pizzas and sausages and beans. He lays aside the carving knife and pours the wine. It is all very civilised.

'So what did you do last night, Sophie?' asks her mother in a friendly voice.

'Nothing much.'

The phone rings then as if on cue and Sophie dives into the hall to answer it, slamming the door behind her. Her chicken and red cabbage and golden potatoes congeal on the plate.

Rachel sighs. 'I don't know what she's up to these days. Fifteen is a ghastly age.'

Cormac could say amen to that, but it could be a mistake.

Clarinda Bain was the youngest pupil in fifth year, though it was difficult to think that she was only fifteen. She looked eighteen at the very least and many of the girls in sixth year could have passed as her junior.

'She has an air of knowingness about her, don't you think?' said Alec McCaffy, when they were having a nightcap together in Cormac's hotel room. He was perched on the only chair, an uncomfortable upright, while Cormac lounged on the bed with his shoes off. His feet ponged a bit but McCaffy would just have to put up with it. His nose was always twitching anyway as if trying to detect bad smells. The students were all asleep, exhausted after a day of non-stop sight-seeing; at least it was to be hoped that they were asleep. The two men had done a little teacherly patrolling along the corridors earlier to make sure that their charges had stayed in their own rooms. What they did back in

Edinburgh was up to them but, here, in their care, they preferred that they didn't indulge in any cohabiting.

Clarinda's name had surfaced in a lazy sort of way.

'An air of confidence, you mean?' said Cormac.

'Of *experience*, I would say. She's been around, don't you think? But she's a likable girl all the same.'

What did Alec mean: all the same? Being liked or disliked surely had nothing to do with having or not having experience? Alec agreed. It was just a *façon de parler*, he said, pleased with himself at bringing out a French phrase. Cormac said, a little pompously, that he did not feel entitled to pass moral judgments on the students. They were not children, these young men and women, though he could not help thinking how immature they were in many ways and uncertain of what they were doing. He thinks the same of his daughter, now that she is the age that Clarinda was then.

# Chapter Six

Kathleen is the next of the aunts to call. She is the hardest edged of the five remaining sisters, not excepting Maeve, Cormac's mother, who, although she likes to 'give off' on the phone, has a softer heart. Kathleen has wiped from her memory those misty, illicit afternoons when she met her married lover along the banks of the river Lagan and takes a hard line now on faithlessness. Perhaps it was because her own lover did not keep faith with her in the end that she has turned this way. She bends the knee at church every morning before she will allow food or drink to cross her lips. She might be doing penance, Cormac has suggested to his mother, who said that the church had become the love of her sister's life. 'She always had to be fixated on something, Kathleen, and there wasn't too much choice left open for her by then. When she was in her teens we thought she might have become a nun.' A bit like Gwen John who in later life turned for solace to the Roman Catholic church? Having lost her revered master, Gwen John took on a new, less troublesome one, who was always there to be spoken to when she wanted to speak to him and who could not jump on a train and escape to Meudon? Her involvement with the church did not seem to have been as all-embracing as his aunt's, however. It appeared to have been somewhat more objective, in that she sketched the nuns and other worshippers in church, which suggests that she was there in part as an observer - are artists always present in part as observers? he wonders - and was not concentrating totally on the mass itself. He finds it odd to be linking the two women in his mind since they stand poles apart in every other way. His aunt has never lived anywhere but Belfast and the only creative thing she ever does is crochet doilies. Though why should he dismiss that? Perhaps she puts her heart and soul in them. Not that that would make them works of art, in his estimation, though some might disagree. His mother, when she responded to his suggestion of his aunt doing penance, said she was sure that Kathleen had long since been redeemed. Lucky Aunt Kathleen.

She is on the phone now, this redeemed aunt, telling him to listen to her. But instead of calling him son she addresses him as Cormac Aherne, which he finds significant. He suspects she is thinking about his father whose surname she often used when addressing him. 'Look here, Patrick Aherne,' she'd say and he'd have his answer ready for her, as smooth as silk, 'I'm all eyes, Kathleen O'Malley, for you're well worth looking at', which would bring a swift blush to her cheeks before she rallied to make her point. Now she says, 'I'm going to give you a good talking to, Cormac Aherne. It's in your own best interests. I'm the one who's always given it to you straight, who's never soft-soaped you.'

He remembers his mother's hard yellow carbolic soap, how brutal it felt against his skin. He used to pinch bars from her cupboard and carve them with his penknife into upright bears and crouching lions. 'You're wasting my good soap!' she'd cry. He'd tell her he wasn't, that he was making something. When he holds a bar of soap in his hands even now he can feel its possibilities, can see it undergoing a transformation, a shape gradually emerging from the mass. He is not careless in his buying of soap; he examines a bar carefully, noting its texture, colour and scent. He likes Pears soap for its lucent amber colour and distinctive smell; it, too, reminds him of childhood for it was the soap that Aunt Sal favoured. His son does not understand his preoccupation; he is not interested in shape or form. He wants to be a doctor when he grows up and have a stethoscope, which he is proud to be able to say correctly. 'That's fine,' Cormac told him. 'Healing people is a good thing. And you'll earn more money than if you were to start carving bars of soap.'

Meanwhile, his aunt is carrying on with her straight talking. Broken marriages are the ruin of society. The children of divorced parents are lost children. 'Away and get back to your wedded wife, son, and no more of this nonsense!'

'What nonsense?'

'Your other woman. And don't be telling me there isn't one!'

He protests in vain, for his aunt isn't listening. She has her own ideas.


Before Cormac and Rachel married they discussed fidelity.

'I don't think so-called 'open marriages' work,' said Rachel. 'I believe in fidelity. I know your father -'

'My father has nothing to do with me,' said Cormac,

which was obviously not true. 'Anyway, my parents' marriage could hardly be described as open! My mother hadn't the faintest idea what he was up to.' They were lying in bed, he and Rachel, a good place to discuss fidelity. He had no intention ever of being unfaithful to her. He smiled and stroked the thick fall of dark hair back from her face. He loved the thickness of her hair, the heavy swing of it against her neck when she moved, just as he loved the direct gaze of her grey eyes which made him think of lake water. He loved everything about her, but especially her calm stillness, some of which he hoped might flow into him, with time. 'I can't imagine being tempted by anyone else when I have you.'

'Maybe not now,' said Rachel seriously. She was a serious person. 'But what about in ten or twenty years time?'

'By then we shall be knee-deep in children.'

They were agreed that they would have children, sometime, and more than one, when their careers were up and running. Rachel had just recently finished her training as a GP and he was trying to make it with his sculpture, eked out by part-time jobs like working in a bar. They were both only children who thought their childhoods would have been better if they'd had siblings; hence their desire for a large family. After having two, they were to change their mind on this.

'Do you think having children will stop one yielding to temptation?' asked Rachel.

He laughed. 'You're not worried, are you?' He kissed the curve of her neck and she twitched at the feel of his mouth on her skin and laughed too.

'No, Cormac, I'm not worried, about anything.' As regards his father's decampment, she couldn't help thinking that she wouldn't blame any man going off and leaving Maeve Aherne and Cormac knew that she thought that. She had a standoffish sort of relationship with his mother which lacked warmth, though they were perfectly polite to each other, and she was careful not to say anything against the woman who would become her mother-in-law, except on the odd occasion when she became exasperated. He'd taken her over to Belfast a couple of times to 'meet the family'. The O'Malley sisters! His mother had put Rachel in the spare room with the glassy pink satin bed cover and curtains to match and the holy pictures on the wall and given him a bed on the settee downstairs. She had left the door of her own room open a chink all night. After one visit Rachel said she could see that Cormac was devoted to his mother, even though he moaned and groaned about her. 'Of course you are! And that's fine by me. She stood by you through the hard years, didn't she, willingly making any sacrifice necessary to give you the chance in life that she didn't have? As you yourself might say, that's not to be sneezed at.' She made him laugh.

They were happy, lying in bed discussing marriage, which they would get round to when it suited them, and fidelity. They talked lazily. It was Sunday morning. Rachel was not on call and he did not have to rush off to work, and they had no children as yet to disrupt their peace. A few weeks after that particular morning Rachel discovered to her astonishment that she was pregnant, something which she had thought she had safely under her control. She was thrown by this for a few days but when she did tell Cormac he was immediately delighted and said they'd better get cracking and tie the knot.

Maeve Aherne, accompanied by her youngest sister, Sal, crossed the Irish Sea for the first time in her life, to come to the wedding of her son, which took place in the suburban Church of Scotland where Rachel's parents worshipped. She was naturally disturbed that he was not being married in the church where he was christened, but such was the way of sons marrying daughters-in-law. As her sisters said to her, daughters-in-law always got their way, and there was nothing she could do to fight that. And, as her son had told her, prior to her coming, if she was going to come she would have to accept what was happening and not criticise. She kept her lip buttoned throughout the ceremony, which she found a poor affair. She disliked the colourlessness of the church, the lack of pomp and ceremony, and she missed the flicker of candles and the smell of incense.

'She seems a nice girl,' said Sal, when the congregation rose at the swelling of *Here Comes the Bride*. Rachel looked beautiful under her floating mist of white, worn to appease her own mother, who was no more charmed by this match than the groom's mother. The bride was led up the aisle by her silver-haired father in morning dress. 'He looks distinguished,' whispered Sal. 'He's obviously not short of a bob or two, You can always tell, can't you?' Rachel's father was a merchant banker, an occupation they had not encountered before but which impressed them. Cormac would appear to be doing all right for himself, said Sal, which mollified his mother to some extent.

'A pity Pat couldn't be here to see him married,' she sighed.

Sal shook her head. Even after so m any years her

sister talked about Pat Aherne as if he had just gone down the road and might turn up at any moment.

On the Friday afternoon that he failed to come home he phoned late in the evening, when he'd have had a drink or two in him to give him the courage, as his wife said afterwards. He was phoning to say he'd been held up.

'Have you a sore throat?' she asked. She was standing in the unheated hall, hunching her shoulders against the chill. Cormac had come half way down the stairs in his pyjamas. When his father hadn't come in he'd had a funny feeling about it. A squirmy sort of feeling low down in his belly. 'Your voice sounds dead queer, Pat,' said his mother. 'As if you're talking through blotting paper.'

She listened for a moment, then looked up at Cormac who was peering through the bannisters. 'He's wanting a word with you, son. Now don't be long. You'll get your death in your bare feet. And you should be asleep in your bed by this time.'

Cormac took the phone while his mother stood waiting.

'Listen, son,' said his father. Cormac was listening intently. 'Something's come up. I can't tell you about it, not yet. Maybe sometime. Be a good lad and look after your mother. I'll see you as soon as I can. And remember your oul' da loves you.'

Cormac put down the receiver and his mother asked, 'What did he say?'

Cormac swallowed and said, 'That he'll be seeing us as soon as he can.'

'I hope he's back by lunch tomorrow. I promised

Mary he'd give her a run up the Antrim Road to her dressmaker's. It'd save her taking two buses.'

But Pat Aherne was not back by lunchtime on Saturday.

'He'll be gassing if I know him,' said his wife. 'Propping up some bar somewhere, spending his hard-earned money.'

But she didn't know him, thought Cormac. He knew his father better than she did.

Aunt Mary came round and had to be disappointed. She sat slumped in a tub chair in the living room complaining about her corns. She'd been relying on a lift. 'My feet are not up to standing waiting on buses so they're not.' She was a large woman with spreading thighs and she wore vast, sack-like dresses with modesty vests at the neck that only partly concealed the deep angry cleft between her bosoms.

'He might be back yet,' said Cormac's mother.

Cormac knew he would not.

'That man of yours never did have any respect for the time, Maeve,' said her sister Mary. 'Or for other people's time, either.'

His wife sprang at once to his defence. She might have a few things to say that were not in his favour but she would not tolerate one word of criticism from her sisters. 'He's a good man. He's always been very obliging. He's obliged you more than once, let me remind you, Mary O'Malley!'

Groaning, Aunt Mary levered herself out of the chair. 'Well, no rest for the wicked.'

She said it, thought Cormac.

'Leave your aunt to the bus stop, Cormac,' said his mother.

After he'd put his aunt on the bus he lingered on the

main road and when he saw Joe Flynn come out of the pub he went over and asked him, 'Would you have seen my daddy at all today?'

'Your daddy, son? No, never set eyes on him. Not last night, neither, and he usually comes in of a Friday. Nothing wrong, is there?'

Cormac shook his head and went on home.

Sunday was one of the longest days of his life. He jumped every time the phone rang but it was always one or other aunts wanting to know if there'd been any sign of his father.

On Monday morning his mother phoned the head office of the shoe polish firm. They'd not heard from Pat Aherne but they presumed he'd be out and about on the job as usual. He was one of their more reliable commercial travellers and they couldn't speak highly enough of him. 'Maybe he was just wanting the weekend off, Mrs Aherne.'

'I could hear the snigger in their voices,' she said to her sister Sal after she'd hung up the receiver.

'Surely they're not thinking he's playing fast and loose with you?' said Sal who, as she said it, suddenly looked thoughtful. She would understand more than any of them the desire to do a bunk.

'He wouldn't do that, not Pat,' said his wife.

After the next weekend passed and Pat Aherne had not checked in, his employers began to take his disappearance more seriously. They suggested to his wife that she should go to the police. He might have had an accident and be lying unconscious in some hospital south of the border. She'd have heard though, wouldn't she? She wasn't keen to go to the police but she didn't know what else to do. Cormac accompanied her up to the station on the main road and she told her story,

119

such as it was, and Cormac told part of what his father had said to him. The constable on the desk noted down the details and said that they'd had no report of any accident that would fit her husband.

'He might turn up yet, Missus. It's early days, just over a week. He might he having himself a wee holiday.'

'Fat lot of use they are,' said Maeve Aherne as they left the station. 'Couldn't find a tram ticket behind their left ear.'

On their return home she decided that they would have to conduct their own investigation. It was out of the question for them to visit all her husband's customers since they had neither money nor transport. They could be contacted, however, by letter or telephone.

They went through Pat Aherne's papers and drew up a list of customers. They were spread far and wide, in places they had heard of and not heard of. Donaghadee, Dundalk, Killarney, Killyleagh, Cookstown, Carlow, Ballymena, Ballybunion...

'Some of these places are at the back-of-beyond,' said Cormac's mother.

Cormac liked the phrase 'back-of-beyond', even though his mother used it deprecatingly. She perceived such places as blanks, unimaginable, and therefore to be dismissed. He saw the grey, misty waters of the lake isle of Innisfree, with nine beans a-growing, and a hive for the honey bee. He heard the gentle lap of the lake water breaking on the shore and the sound of linnets' wings filling the evening air. *The Lake Isle of Innisfree* had been one of his father's favourite poems. 'Wouldn't it be great,' his father had said on one occasion, 'to find a place where peace comes dropping slow?' Cormac wondered now if his father had found such a place and if so he might send for him and they could plant the bean rows together and live in the bee-loud glade.

'He was a well-travelled man right enough,' said Pat Aherne's wife, as if he was dead. 'It could take us weeks getting through this lot.'

It took them a full week. Most of the customers were on the phone; only a scattering of small village shops were not but these Pat Aherne had visited only once a year, so his records told them. To these Cormac penned careful letters on his mother's lilac-tinted, lined notepaper that had sprigs of violets in the top left-hand corner and on the matching envelopes. His mother dictated: 'Dear sir or madam, I believe my husband Pat Aherne, who travels in shoe polish, calls at your premises. He has not been home recently and I am worried in case he has met with an accident or is suffering from loss of memory. If you have seen him in the last three weeks I would be most grateful if you would contact me at the above address. Yours faithfully.'

'You sign my name, Cormac.'

Cormac signed 'Maeve Aherne' in backward, sloping writing, to make it look unlike his own, which was firm and upright. In school he was complimented on his fine, clear handwriting. 'You have a good hand, Cormac,' his teacher told him.

His mother got him to make the phone calls too. 'I don't like the phone,' she said, though she spoke to her sisters on it every day. But that was different from talking to total strangers whose faces she couldn't imagine. Later, Cormac would come to wonder if it was the making of these calls which made him hate the telephone so violently. His mother had another reason for asking

121

him to do it, of which he was aware; she was too proud to tell these people, 'My husband hasn't come home.'

For the first few calls his throat was dry and he had to keep clearing it but after that it was as if it was oiled and the questions slipped smoothly out. 'I wonder if by any chance you might have seen my dad Pat Aherne recently?' For a minute or two he would then nurse the receiver while the person at the other end extolled on the likability of Pat Aherne. 'He's great crack, Pat, so he is. We always look forward to him coming. He cheers you up so he does.' And then, 'But, no, we've not seen him this last month or so. Is there anything wrong? I hope nothing's happened to him. Hang on a minute till I get Maureen. She might be able to tell you when he was last here.'

Cormac held the receiver against his chest.

'What's going on?' asked his mother.

'He's gone to ask Maureen.'

'This'll be be costing us a fortune. Maureen could be anywhere, whoever Maureen is.'

In due time, Maureen herself came to the phone. 'Are you Cormac, Pat's wee lad? How are you, son? I hope nothing's happened to your daddy. He was always talking about you, telling us how clever you were, especially with your hands. He's not been here for a wee while now. I was expecting him in last week, as a matter of fact. Our stocks are running low. A woman was just in there looking for ox-blood and I couldn't oblige her. Will you be taking orders yourself? Or your mammy?'

Not right now, he told her, and hung up.

His mother had her finger under the next number on the list. She read and he dialled. He dialled Tralee and Galway, Newry and Portrush, Dublin and Donegal town. He began to feel he was travelling Ireland himself.

And then, one evening, he got his first lead.

'Your dad was in one Thursday there, two or three weeks back,' said the man at the other end of the line. 'Hang on and I'll go and check my order book.' When he returned he was able to tell Cormac that his father had visited his shop on the Thursday of the week before he disappeared. 'After that he was heading up into Clare.'

Cormac dialled a County Clare number on the list and a woman answered. She knew Cormac for once his father had taken him on a trip over to the west and they had called at her shop and she had given him a large bag of bulls' eyes. 'We saw your daddy not that long ago, on a Thursday it was. I remember it was a Thursday for my sister always comes for her lunch on a Thursday. She lives out in the country, you see, and it's her day for the butcher. I'd bought a nice bit of liver so I said to your dad that he was welcome to join us. 'I've plenty,' I told him 'and liver's good for the blood." When the woman's memory was jogged further she pin-pointed the week.

'We're getting there,' Cormac told his mother. He felt excited and sick at the same time.

Only one County Clare number remained on the list. This man also recalled meeting Cormac and was able to tell him that his father had been in on the Friday of that week and that he'd been in great form. He didn't know where he was heading afterwards. 'Mrs Blaney might be able to tell you. He stayed there on the Thursday night.'

Mrs Blaney was a widow woman who lived about

five miles out of the village, up a rough track. She took in the odd B&B when the chance arose, which was not too often in such a remote spot. There was not a lot of passing trade. Cormac had spent a night there with his father. She'd welcomed him with open arms, gathering him to her soft, pillowy bosom. For a moment he'd thought he was going to suffocate until he managed to ease his face away. 'He's a nice looking lad, Pat,' she'd said. 'A chip off the old block!' She had a full-throated laugh. She'd given them a great tea of thick cut ham and fried potatoes with apple pie to follow and two kinds of cake. Cormac had stuffed himself full and had then fallen asleep in front of the warm peat fire, scarcely surfacing when his father had carried him through to the bedroom.

The County Clare shopkeeper gave Cormac the phone number of Mrs Blaney, while commenting that he hadn't seen her for a bit. 'She might be off visiting her sisters in Galway. It's a bit lonely for her in that house there, with her man gone.'

Cormac thanked the shopkeeper. His ear was getting hot and sore from pressing it against the receiver rim. He dialled this last number, knowing that it would be the last. He heard the phone ringing at the other end, remembered the the comforting warmth of the slow-burning peat fire, and the pleasure of the sweet, moist cakes, and wakening in the morning into a calm stillness broken only by a few plaintive bird notes and Mrs Blaney's soft, pillowy laugh coming from another room.

The phone went on ringing, and on ringing, and on ringing.

'There's no one there,' he said to his mother and wiped his damp hand against his jersey sleeve.

To Maeve Aherne, her husband's disappearance remained a mystery, for her son said not a word to her about the secret things he knew. Pat Aherne was not seen again by them, nor by the shoe-polish firm who would have liked to recover their car and their samples of shoe-polish. They sent threatening letters to his wife. She had done nothing with the car, Cormac wrote back, acting once again as her scribe, and she had no money to give them in compensation. The very idea! The boot should be on the other foot. They should be compensating her for sending her husband into wild and lonely places. Goodness knows, he might be lying in a bog, for all they knew!

Cormac and his mother were poor now. The days of sliders and sand castles at Donaghadee belonged to the past. Maeve Aherne got a job in a greengrocer's but it didn't go anywhere near compensating for the loss of her husband's income. She brought home a bag of tired vegetables at the end of each day and just enough money at the weekend to pay the rent and insurance and get basic shopping at the Co-Op.

Before their telephone was taken away, Cormac tried Mrs Blaney's number once more, when his mother was out. This time there was no ringing tone, only a long note that sounded like a dirge. He felt sure his father was no longer in the country. He would have crossed the Irish Sea, gone to the mainland. The sea was a great divide; it offered a means of escape, which, in his own good time, Cormac himself would take.

Aunt Kathleen is still on the phone waiting for a response from his end.

'Why should you think there's another woman, Aunt Kathleen?' he asks, a little slyly.

'There always is.' She should know, right enough!

'Or man,' he puts in. But perhaps she has forgotten that part of her life, effaced it from her memory.

She does not react but goes on to tell him that his mother has need of him. 'She'll never admit it, Cormac, but she's going downhill. You'll see a difference. She's frail these days.'

For a while after Cormac's father disappeared postal orders made out to Maeve Aherne arrived in envelopes posted and registered in various towns and cities of England. First, there was Liverpool, for wasn't that where many Irishmen ended up, with no money to take them further? Pat Aherne did travel on for after that came Walsall and then Wigan and Warrington. There was never an address to write back to.

'He always did have itchy feet,' his wife commented. 'I should have seen the signal when we were courting. He was always talking about going to America. But then a lot of them talk that way, don't they, and they never go?'

It might only have been the north and the Midlands of England Pat Aherne had absconded to but for all the difference it made to them it might as well have been America.

'Towns beginning with W,' said his son, bent over a map of England, trying to fathom where his father might go next. Wolverhampton? That was further south, but it might take his fancy.

Pat's next port-of-call turned out to be Coventry, breaking the pattern, and after that there was a long silence. Then came a letter saying, 'Hope you are both keeping well', with a five pound note inside it.

'Not worth him getting an order for, I suppose,' said his wife, who by this time expected nothing.

Nothing else came.

After his phone call from Aunt Kathleen Cormac feels he has no option but to ring his mother. 'I'll be over at Easter,' he promises.

As soon as he puts the phone down he goes upstairs to tell Davy that they will be going to Belfast for the Easter holidays; stating it will help to cement his will. Davy is lying on the bed, face down.

'What's up, son?' He sits on the bed beside the boy and strokes his hair.

'Nothing.'

'Come now, there is, so tell me,' says Cormac softly. He feels soft where his son is concerned. His daughter, too. Rachel was always telling him he was too soft with them. Too soft for their own good. It wasn't doing them a favour; they'd grow up to find the world a harder place than they'd imagined. 'You know you can tell me anything that's bothering you, Davy,' says his father. 'And if I can do anything about it, I will.'

The boy lifts his head. His face is red and blotchy and his blond hair is sticking out like wisps of straw, which makes Cormac's heart turn over. He would do anything to protect this child.

Davy wipes his eyes with the back of his sleeve. ' I'm just missing my mum,' he says and the tears come afresh.

Cormac cries, too, over the top of his son's head as he hugs him to his chest and rocks him, the way he did when was smaller. He's still small. What terrible things are they doing to the children! And yet, what else were they to do? Their situation before had become untenable and this had seemed a civilised solution: sharing the children, living a couple of streets away from one another, spending Sundays together, like a family. It's all right for Aunt Kathleen to say, 'Away back to your wife!'

They lay in bed together, he and Rachel, on the night after his suspension from school, not touching, a clear gap between them, each keeping, by mutual, unspoken agreement, to their own side, as if they had thoughts they wished to keep separate from the other. Archie Gibson's words still trembled in his head. 'I have no option, Cormac -' No option. No option.

'Are you awake?' asked Rachel, her voice quiet.

'Yes.'

'There's something I should tell you, Cormac.'

He tensed, sensing from the vibration in her voice that this would be something he would not wish to hear. A car passed in the street, its tyres swishing softly on the wet tarmac. Possibly a neighbour coming home. Ah yes, that was what it was. The engine had cut out, car doors were slamming. All common night-time, reassuring sounds, except that tonight nothing could reassure him, except for a phone call from Mrs Bain to tell him that they were withdrawing their complaint and that it had all been a terrible mistake. But that was unlikely. Mrs Bain had gone too far for that and she was not a woman prepared to suffer loss of face. And she wanted him to suffer. She wanted to ruin him. He had offended her, had he not?

'I've been having an affair,' said Rachel. 'It didn't last long, and it's over now. We were only together two or three times. I'm sorry.'

He was stunned. It had never occurred to him that Rachel - *Rachel*, of all people ... He couldn't believe that she had been as intimate with another man as she had been with him.

'I'm sorry,' she repeated. 'Especially having to tell you this today. But somehow I had to, I don't know why. Or perhaps it's because of what happened today. I want to be open with you. We've got to be open with each other. And I didn't want you to hear any rumours from anywhere else - just in case.'

In case they had been seen together? Though Rachel would have been very careful, he was sure, very discreet, whatever she had been doing. But no one could afford to discount chance. Had someone seen them, this man, whoever he might be, and her, when they had least expected it? Was that the reason for her confession? *By the way, Cormac, I saw your wife with ...* With *whom*? His brain felt befuddled and incapable of taking anything more in.

She was lying on her back, eyes wide open, staring at the ceiling. Was she waiting for him to make a similar confession? He did have a sin, a minor one, he rated it, but still a transgression that surfaced every now and then to cause him unease. He had been unfaithful to Rachel following the birth of Sophie. He'd gone out with some mates to celebrate and had drunk a skinful and they'd picked up or been picked up by some women out on a hen night. Somehow or other he had ended up with one of them in her bed. Afterwards, it had all seemed rather foolish, but he hadn't dared tell

Rachel in case she would leave him and take their beautiful new baby with her. Could he face telling her now? His brief fling would seem tawdry beside her serious affair. For he did not doubt that hers would have been serious; Rachel would not embark on such a thing lightly. That was what bothered him more than anything: he feared she might have fallen in love with someone else.

He felt as if his marriage was coming apart, unravelling between his hands, like a piece of worn-out cloth. One false move, or word, and it would be rent asunder.

He ran his tongue over his parched lips and told her. She was very quiet, she hardly seemed to be breathing. Did she feel that his transgression evened the score? He thought not.

'Things haven't been very good between us for a while, have they?' she said eventually.

'Haven't they?' he responded stubbornly, though he knew that what she was saying was true. They had been drifting away from each other a little, but perhaps that was understandable after so many years. It didn't mean that he didn't still love her.

'You're upstairs every night, night after night, in your studio. Wrapped up in your sculpture. I know that when you start working on something you can't think of anything else. But I hardly ever see you, except at mealtimes and even then you're only half there.'

So she resented his work, did she? But he couldn't live without it, he'd wither away. He had always thought she supported him, was proud of him even; she'd said so when he had his recent exhibition.

'I suppose I am a bit caught up in it,' he muttered.

'Obsessed, I'd say. But then maybe you have to be to achieve anything.'

130

'But you're often out yourself in the evening. At your meetings and classes.' She was a school governor and she went to conversation classes at the French Institute and to aerobic classes and sometimes she had a night out with her women friends. They had always agreed it was good to have separate interests, not to live in each other's pockets.

'But I'm not out till one or two am. I don't come to bed in the middle of the night and get up in the morning growling like a bear with a sore head. You know you're often grumpy in the morning because you haven't slept enough.'

'So it's my fault, is it? That you've been having an affair?' He still couldn't make sense of it. That Rachel, whom he thought he knew almost as well as he knew himself, and who was usually honest and rational and reasonable, should do something that seemed so out of character. But what did it mean 'out of character'? Only that someone was taking you by surprise.

'Of course it's not your fault!' she said almost sharply. 'I'm not trying to put the blame on you. I'm just trying to understand where we are.'

They are silent, each locked once more inside their own thoughts.

He swallowed and asked, 'Who is he, anyway?'

'That's of no importance.'

'No importance!' He sat up. 'For Christ's sake, how can you say that?'

'It's over,' she said again. But could he believe her?

# Chapter Seven

Cormac leaves Davy and runs back down the stairs. He lifts the receiver. He seems to spend half his evenings on the telephone these days, which he didn't do when he was with Rachel; she took charge of it then, calling him only if it was his mother or one of the aunts. But they call more often, these female relatives of his, now that they do not have to go through Rachel, not that she would be unfriendly to them, she'd always have a little chat, ask after their health, before running up the two flights of stairs to bang on his studio door. From his high retreat he had been blessed by only being able to hear the phone ringing distantly. In this small house it penetrates every corner.

He dials Rachel's number and waits. He is going to have to give her the satisfaction of telling her that Davy wants her. The boy's welfare takes priority over his petty pride. Davy can go and spend the night with her if he wishes, and he does. 'It's not a problem,' he told him before coming downstairs. 'You can go round any time you want to.' As long as he comes back to him: that he leaves unspoken. It is not a clause he can insist on.

The answering machine is coming on, drat the bloody thing! *This is the answering machine for Sophie and*

*Rachel Aherne. We're sorry* ... Ta, ra, ta, ra. He clamps the receiver back onto its rest, cutting off her well-modulated voice. Oh, yes, he bets she's sorry. Where the hell is she when her son is crying for her upstairs? Out with her lover? He knows he's being unreasonable and would acknowledge that he often is, but ever since Rachel told him about her affair he has been obsessed by the identity of this man who lured her into his arms. Or perhaps she lured him into hers? Now he's being ridiculous. He can imagine her voice telling him so. But is he?

She might be on call, he tells himself, at the bedside of a sick child. She might be at the French Institute making conversation about holidays spent in converted farmhouses in the valleys of the Lot and the Dordogne. She might be at the cinema watching a French film. But Sophie is not at home either and she should be, doing her homework. Her GCSEs are coming up. Is she doing any work for them? He asked Rachel the last time they talked - there was no point in asking Sophie - and she confessed, not an awful lot. But how do you make someone who doesn't want to work work? How do you keep a fifteen-year-old in the house unless you tie her up or lock her in her room and if you were to do that she would probably climb down the drainpipe. And then she might run away from home. She might go on the streets, fall in with a crowd of druggies. His imagination is running away with itself, as his mother used to tell him when he exaggerated. Just like your da, she'd tell him. Pat Aherne was known for his stories. A little embroidery here and there doesn't do a pick of harm, he'd say; it adds a bit of spice. Cormac is sorry Sophie hasn't had the chance to know her grandfather; he thinks she would have enjoyed his crack.

Rachel thinks Sophie might need to learn a lesson. If she fails her exams, so be it. Sophie doesn't like to fail; she has always been competitive, so that might bring her to her senses. On the other hand, her father thinks that if she does miserably badly at her GCSEs she might leave school and get work chopping vegetables in Henderson's kitchen and describe it as honest toil, which it may be, but he wants his daughter to live up to herself, to realise her potential, though he knows he would be on rocky ground, given his own situation, if he were to make much of that.

It would help if her mother was in the house, encouraging her, listening to her French verbs. What *is* Rachel up to? She has absolutely refused to tell him with whom she was having an affair. Was? Is she still? She finds it easy to keep secrets, whereas he does not. He suspects an old boyfriend of hers who reappeared in Edinburgh after years spent in the steamy jungles of Guatemala; one of the doctors in the practice who is a bachelor; the man who used to live next door to them and who always referred to her as 'your charming wife' whenever Cormac talked to him. No, he thinks he can rule the last one out; she can't be that gormless. And maybe the unmarried doctor might not be interested in women at all. There don't seem to be too many choices left and the one from the jungle went back there, he seems to recall. He wishes he had paid more attention when Rachel talked about him.

After she'd told him about her affair he found it difficult to touch her and when he did he thought of the other, unknown man touching her. And perhaps she thought of him too. He became obsessed by thoughts of that other man, all the more so, he did not doubt, because he had so little else to fill his imagination, apart from his own predicament. It was the waiting that got to him most of all, wakening each morning to wonder if they would come for him today. He almost welcomed this further obsession, in that it crowded out the other for periods of time. His mind bounced between Clarinda Bain and his wife's ex-lover. Ex? Whenever the phone rang he would run half way down the stairs and listen but he never heard anything of significance. Suspicions, though, continued to buzz in his head like an angry posse of flies, and still do. The unspoken suspicions on both sides added to the tension in the house. They were both as taut as piano wire. They snapped at each other over trivialities and then apologised too quickly, like strangers who have collided in the street.

Rachel, though, did her best to see him through this terrible time. A kindly woman, she cared about her patients, and him, too. That was one thing he did not doubt. She said, 'It will all pass, Cormac, you'll see, and then everything will settle down again. I'll always stand by you. And don't mention Tammy Wynette!' She smiled, trying to lighten the moment.

He had little faith in the idea of everything settling down. After a cyclone passed there was bound to be debris left behind.

'I believe in you,' she said, but could he believe that she did? He was racked by disbelief.

He was taken into the police station again for questioning and then released. But came the day that the Procurator Fiscal decided he had a case to answer. He was summoned back to the police station where he was formally charged with sexual harassment of a minor and warned that anything he might say could be taken down and given in evidence against him. He had no wish to say anything, once he had acknowledged that he was Cormac Patrick Aherne and that he lived at a certain address. He felt no surprise as he stood stiffly there, listening to the wooden police voice. All was going as he had imagined. It was Rachel who had been optimistic, or had purported to be, who had said, 'They'll drop it, you'll see. They haven't a leg to stand on.' But they obviously thought that the ground was firm beneath their feet though they appeared not to regard him as a menace to the community at large for they allowed him bail. Rachel, who had accompanied him to the station, prepared to leave to raise the bail money from her father.

'Is there no other way?' he muttered. It seemed that his humiliation would be without limit.

'None. You know we haven't anything to speak of in the bank.' They lived, like most people, up to the limits of their earning power, sometimes running just a little into the red.

'I won't be long,' said Rachel and left.

What if they wouldn't give it to her? But they would; for her sake, not his.

His lawyer was a pal of her father, reputed to be one of Edinburgh's best. He said, 'Don't worry, Cormac, old chap. We'll squash Miss Clarinda Bain's testimony in court. Is there anything you know about her - or could you suggest anyone who might know anything - that would help?'

'In what way?'

137

'Well, to be blunt - and in a situation like this one can only be blunt - something that would cast aspersions on her character. Sexual, preferably.'

'You mean, throw dirt at her? Make her out to be some sort of trollop?' That was a word from his mother's vocabulary! It had slipped out from the recesses of his mind.

'And what do you think she's making you out to be? A seducer of young girls! Look, Cormac, it's either you or her the court is going to believe. If you're found not guilty all that will happen to her is that she'll go away with her tail between her legs and think twice before making allegations in future. But if you are found guilty you will go to prison. And what do you think that would do to Rachel and the children? Lovely woman, Rachel. Bright, too. Head girl at her school and all that. Did brilliantly at university. She could have become a consultant instead of a G.P. but having children did rather scupper that, didn't it? You're a lucky man, Cormac.' Cormac had always been aware that Rachel's parents and their friends had thought she could have done better for herself.

Afterwards, Rachel drove him home and they stayed for a few moments in the car before going into the house.

'I take it that you never touched her?' she said. 'Or gave her any encouragement?'

He paused before he answered. 'Not consciously, at any rate.' It was the best that he could do.

She pursed her lips then swung open her door and stepped out onto the pavement.

'Did she say I could come?' Davy puts his head round the door.

'She's not in, I'm afraid.'

'Not in?' Davy's voice begins to waver again.

'Come on, lad, let's go out and paint the town pink!'

They go to Henderson's Salad Bar where a man is tinkling on the piano and no one is listening. How demoralising, thinks Cormac, whose own morale sags when a customer eats but a couple of bites out of one of his sandwiches and trashes the rest in the outside bin. But perhaps the pianist does not care about approbation; his only need might be to play. Davy eats trifle and Cormac drinks red wine and broods. Rachel is entitled to go out with whom she pleases, he tells himself. He has no rights over her. They have separated. Parted. He feels far apart from her yet he cannot let her go.

'Hello, Cormac.'

He feels a shadow over him and looks up to see Clarinda Bain looking down at him. Can she be following him? She is with another girl tonight, one that he vaguely recognises, and they are carrying trays of salad aloft.

She rests her tray on the corner of his table. 'How are you?'

'Why do you ask?'

'I don't know.' She looks at Davy. 'Is this your son?'

He has to acknowledge Davy to her. Davy gives her a blank stare - he mercifully has never heard of Clarinda Bain - and asks if he can get himself another glass of orange juice. Cormac automatically gives him the money and he goes off to the counter.

'I'm sorry about everything, you know,' says Clarinda.

'You're spilling your salad.' Coleslaw is running over from the edge of her plate into the tray.

'Are you coming, Clarrie?' her friend calls over.

139

'Better go,' he says.

His hand shakes as he raises his glass to his mouth. He would have liked to have thrown the wine over her but he would not have been able to summon the energy had he tried.

Next day, when he is clearing up in the shop, before going to fetch Davy, she comes in. He goes on washing the floor.

'Won't you talk to me, Cormac?'

'Get lost, Clarinda, *please!*'

'What does it all matter now?'

'Now that I'm no longer a teacher and you're no longer my pupil? And now that I'm no longer married.'

'I heard you'd left your wife.'

'I didn't leave her. We left each other, by mutual consent. Now, if you don't mind, I'll get on with my work.' He rinses the mop in the bucket and squeezes out the water as tightly as he can. The muscles in his upper arm bulge. 'I'm trying to wash the mayonnaise and mustard off the floor so that my customers won't slip and fall on their rear ends when they come in the door tomorrow.'

'It's terrible that someone like you should be making sandwiches!'

'I'd rather do it than stand on a corner and sell *The Big Issue.*' He makes a wide sweep near her feet and she has to jump back.

'Cormac, why don't you go back to your sculpting?'

'Do you think that would feed me and my son? Anyway, it's finished. It's gone dead on me. Objects look dead. I'm opting for the living now. That's why I'm into feeding them, seeing them go out the door and return the next day smacking their lips, satisfied, repeat customers. When you're an artist you don't have as many satisfied customers, certainly not on a daily basis. You spend days, weeks, months, soldiering on, alone, wondering if you're mental to carry on.'

'It's not to do with customers,' she cries and he thinks she might be about to stamp her foot. 'It's not a business proposition.'

She has listened well to his lectures, too well, for now she can throw his words back in his face. She was a good student, one of the best he ever had.

'Look,' he says, 'I'm running late. I have to be at my son's school on time so, for God's sake, Clarinda, get out of my bloody way!'

On the Saturday of their stay in Paris they went to the Marché aux Puces. Today, art was out, commerce was in. The pupils were excited on the long Métro ride out to Clignancourt and were counting their money and talking about bargains.

'Be careful you don't get taken for a ride,' warned Cormac. 'The place is full of chancers, as well as pickpockets.'

He sat beside one of the boys and they talked football. He thought he might have been pushing art too much; now was the time for a little leavening. He knew himself that there was only so much one could look at at a time; after that point was passed nothing much was retained. He had yet to visit the Louvre successfully. But the Rodin Museum now, that was different. He could go back time after time, and on this trip had gone three times. Not all the pupils had come with him. Clarinda Bain was the only one who had come every time.

The flea market was thronged with touts and tourists as well as natives.

'It won't be possible for us all to stay together in this crush,' said Alec. He split them into small groups of three and four, appointing the most responsible in each as leader, and told them to return to the starting point afterwards. He was an excellent organiser.

Cormac took his small squad into the heart of the market. They trawled through rails of leather coats and cheap jeans and tee-shirts and poked in boxes of old postcards and sepia-coloured photographs and tangled jewellery and ceramic door knobs and moth-eaten feather boas. They bought a few odds and ends, not much. They didn't have much money left by this stage; there was only more day to go after this, a fact they were bemoaning already. Cormac had been amazed how much money some of the students had had at the start. Clarinda had had less than most; he got the impression that she and her mother were quite hard up. Mrs Bain worked part-time in an antique shop and helped out a friend who ran a second-hand clothes shop that sold 'designer labels'. Cormac presumed that most of Mrs Bain's dramatic wardrobe came from this source.

Clarinda, who was part of his group, bought herself a long string of blue beads that were the colour of gentians. She wore them when they were having lunch out there at Clignancourt, at a *café concert* called *Chez Louisette* and billed as *La dernière guingette de Paris*. 'What do you think, Cormac?' she asked him, twirling the strand of beads round her long slender fingers. The pupils had started to call Alec and himself by their Christian names after the first day. They were mostly seventeen years old, and in their last year at school, so it did seem daft for them to have to go on referring to them as Mr This and Mr That. The relationship between teacher and pupil was becoming more casual by the day, the dividing line more blurred. He had noticed her hands before. How could he not? He noticed the hands of all his students. They were of interest to him. He watched them as they worked and learned from watching.

Clarinda was sharing his table, along with another girl and boy, a couple, who were having a problem keeping their hands off each other. Cormac suspected they were spending their nights together. He and Alec had discussed the matter but had decided to ignore it since the pair had been a couple long before they ever came to Paris. After seeing *The Kiss*, Robbie had dubbed them Paolo and Francesca, which had embarrassed them but had not stopped them from locking themselves into tight embraces whenever possible.

'The beads match your eyes,' Cormac told Clarinda, which pleased her.

They were in the upstairs gallery of the restaurant, occupying several tables. The place was packed and the atmosphere hectic. People were queuing in the narrow alleyway outside while perspiring waitresses ran to and fro slapping down plates of food and whipping the white paper covers off the yellow undercloths the instant a table was vacated. When the concert got into full swing they had to scream their orders to be heard above the deafening sound system. Meanwhile, the proprietors, Armand and Richard, looking like twins with similar glasses and moustaches, stood below, perfectly composed; or so they appeared.

143

The first singer was a woman who was going to *chante Piaf.* She stepped up to the dais wearing a grey trouser suit and stilettos, looking much more vigorous than Piaf had ever been. This woman would be able to take care of herself; there was nothing waif-like about her. Her short hair was grey and her orange make-up had been lavishly applied. Her voice, when she began to sing, had the harsher notes of Piaf's voice, though not its pathos, but she knew how to give the audience what it wanted. *Je ne regrette rien* ... She rolled her rs well. Cheers rang out, feet pumped on the floor. 'This is great!' Clarinda's eyes were shining. She had drunk two or three glasses of cheap red wine, as had all the students. Cormac was enjoying himself too. He liked when things went over the top and entered the realm of camp. It was fun. Piaf's stand-in reeled off all her best known numbers and received rapturous applause, after which she came round with her little basket looking for offerings.

They were then treated to a rather paunchy man taking up the baton to *chante Paris. Sous les ponts de Paris* ... The audience swayed in time with him and some sang along, the women in the audience mostly, smiling to themselves, remembering past moments. Following him came a guitarist, gypsyish, with wild dark locks and a gyrating belly, aping Elvis. After he had come round with his basket and the restaurant had subsided a little Cormac noticed they had finished their litre carafe of wine and ordered another.

'I have definitely made up my mind,' said Clarinda, 'I am going to come to Paris after I finish at art college.'

'Every day won't be like this.'

'I wouldn't expect it to. But I could come here and

sketch some of the people.' She had a talent for catching the essence of a person in her drawing.

The other two at their table were so totally absorbed that he and Clarinda had no option but to converse together, as he said to Alec later, when they were discussing the day and Alec said, 'You and Miss Bain seemed to be having a real *tête-a-tête*. Heads together, eh!' 'No other way to be heard in that madhouse,' Cormac retorted. That was what he would say when he came to be investigated, using slightly different words, expanding a little so that they, his interrogators, would get the picture.

*We were told, Mr Aherne, that on that visit to the flea market at Clignancourt you appeared to be talking intimately with the girl in question. Tête-a-tête, would that describe it?*

It must have been Alec McCaffy who so described it, but if he were to ask they would not reveal their sources. It didn't take much to work it out, however. He might have said, though did not, that he had seen Mr McCaffy *tête-a-tête* with a girl called Effie who was going to university next year to do geography, so that Mr McCaffy had a special interest in her, just as he had in Clarinda Bain, who was going to study art. But all that was yet to come.

After they had settled the bill, which came to more than they had anticipated, and left the restaurant, the students were in boisterous mood. They sang *Je ne regrette rien* at the tops of their voices, exaggerating their words and gestures. Alec hoped they were not too drunk. Cormac told him not to worry. 'They can take it. I bet they can sink a lot more at their own parties. They're just in high spirits, intoxicated by the scene as much as the wine.'

145

Clarinda wanted to go back to the booth where she had bought her necklace; she had seen one that she thought that her mother would like, in jade green.

'You can't go off on your own,' objected Alec. They had a rule that no student was allowed to go alone anywhere, even to the small grocer-cum-greengrocer across the street from their hotel. 'It's like a maze, this place, you could get lost without trying.'

Cathy and Sue wanted to buy something that they had also seen earlier and suggested that the three of them go together. Cormac volunteered to accompany them. 'You go on ahead, Alec,' he said, 'and we'll catch you up. Wait for us at the Metro if we don't see you before then.'

Alec led the rest of the students away and it was unfortunate that two of them chose to throw up just seconds after they parted. They deposited the undigested aftermath of their *poulet et frites* lunch, washed down with *vin rouge*, over the merchandise of a carpet seller. Half a dozen Afghan rugs had been liberally spattered. Mayhem broke out, with the carpet seller dancing with rage and screaming profanities (at least Alec presumed that was what they were) and neighbouring stall holders coming running to join in and shout, also of course in French, which Alec had little understanding of, except for the word *compensation*. *Compensation pour le nettoyage.* For the cleaning, a girl, who was studying for a French Higher, translated for him.

'Run back and get Cormac, quick!' he instructed one of the boys. Cormac could speak French reasonably well.

But by then it was too late for Cormac and his group

146

had vanished down one of the many alleyways and the boy himself almost got lost trying to make his way back. Alec had to try to sort out his own mess. The girl who was doing the French Higher tried to negotiate with the carpet man but she said she couldn't make out his accent; also, he kept shouting, which didn't help. The only thing Alec could think to do was to open his wallet and offer a hundred franc note. It was tossed aside. *Une insulte*! He did get that one, too. Several students scrambled after the note, almost getting themselves kicked on the head by onlookers. A couple of the girls were becoming semi-hysterical, giggling uncontrollably. More screaming and dancing on the spot by the carpet seller ensued until six hundred francs was raised and they were allowed to pass. Until then their way had been solidly blocked at both ends. As Alec led them out of the market towards the Métro he swore that he would never again take a party of students abroad. He reckoned they'd got off relatively lightly with sixty quid, though it did leave them rather short, and of course one of the students would be stupid enough when they got back to tell her mother and the mother would come up to complain to the headmaster. One way and another, their trip to Paris was to achieve notoriety.

Cormac and the three girls had meanwhile gone on their way looking for the booths that they had seen earlier, which were more difficult to locate than they had anticipated. They made a few false turnings before Cathy and Sue found what they were looking for. Clarinda said she thought hers was just round the corner. Cormac told the other two girls to come and get them as soon as they'd done their shopping.

Clarinda couldn't find the booth round the first corner, yet she could have sworn that that was where it had been. They tried the next one and there it was and the necklace that she thought her mother would like. She bought it without any fuss; the transaction couldn't have taken more than five minutes, after which they returned to the place where they had left Cathy and Sue, but of them there was no sign. They must have taken a wrong turning themselves. Cormac and Clarinda set out to look for them, stopping at one or two booths so that Cormac could ask if anyone had seen two girls, one with short blond hair, the other reddish-brown and curly, about the same height as the girl he was with, speaking English. No one could recollect girls of that description but there were many people about, so many girls, of all kinds and colours. Who would notice anyone in particular in such a crowd?

Cormac and Clarinda found themselves back at *Chez Louisette*.

'Could I have a coffee?' asked Clarinda. 'I think I need to sober up.' She giggled.

*It sounds, Mr Aherne, as if you allowed the pupils to consume rather a large quantity of red wine? And then, after the lunch, how come you were on your own with the girl in question?*

The restaurant had only a few customers since the afternoon was drawing to a close and most of those who wished to lunch had already done so. They sat at a downstairs table and drank black coffee and were serenaded once more with *chansons de Paris*. Elvis seemed to have knocked off. Cormac was beginning to wish that he could himself but he had two missing students to find.

*You say you got separated from the other two girls, Mr Aherne? Was it not your responsibility to see that that did not happen?*

They didn't find them for the reason, simple enough, that the girls had managed to link up with the rest of the group and had continued with them to the Métro station where they had waited for ten minutes to see if Cormac and Clarinda would appear. When they did not, Alec decided that they should not wait any longer since the two who had vomited were miserable in their smelly shirts and trainers and two, who had not yet vomited, were feeling that they might.

*It seems odd, Mr Aherne, that the other two girls who had got separated from the main party managed to join up with it again yet, you, who had been at this flea market before and could speak French, failed to do so.*

Cormac and Clarinda searched until the shopkeepers and stall holders were packing up.

'We'd best head back,' said Cormac, 'and see if Sue and Cathy have got there before us.'

When they reached the Métro station they saw no sign either of the two girls or of anyone else from their group. A Romany woman sat on the ground near the entrance nursing a wan-faced baby.

*'Que belle!'* She grinned at Clarinda, opening her mouth to display a few broken teeth at the front.

Clarinda immediately pulled out her purse and thrust some francs into the woman's hand.

'Was that wise?' murmured Cormac.

He had no sooner spoken than they were set upon by a number of other clamouring gypsy women and girls who appeared as if out of nowhere. Cormac tried to flap them aside as he might a posse of buzzing flies but they were persistent, and in the end he and Clarinda had to take to their heels and outrun them. He noticed Clarinda's bare arms were scratched.

'It's nothing,' she said with a shrug. 'They're poor.'

'I know.'

Suddenly he realised that at this moment he was not so well off himself. He had used the last of his money to settle the lunch bill. 'Got any cash on you?'

Clarinda shook her head without engaging his eye. She had given her last franc to the woman.

What to do now, wondered Cormac, who felt like a drink more than anything else. They had bought carnets of Métro tickets for the group but Alec had those in the red knapsack he carried on his back.

'We'll just have to walk then, won't we?' said Clarinda brightly.

'It's a long way,' said Cormac gloomily. 'We're right out at the *périphérique* that runs round the outside rim of Paris.'

They had no map, either; that was also in Alec's backpack.

'We wouldn't need a map, would we?' Clarinda sounded amazingly bright. At fifteen, not quite sixteen, the thought of walking all those miles through the streets of Paris was probably attractive. An adventure. This was when he began to be aware that he had passed forty some time ago.

'I guess not. If we keep heading south.'

They set out, down the long Boulevard Omano. God, Paris boulevards could be long and straight and grey. Clarinda loped along enthusing about Paris and how her mother had said she would. Mrs Bain had herself come as a girl and fallen madly in love with the city. He felt uncomfortable when Clarinda talked about her mother; it conjured up images of the woman moving in on him with scarlet-tipped nails and a pungent smell of perfume. From Omano they changed to the Boulevard Barbes, equally long and straight. He had been insistent that the pupils should walk as much as possible around the city, Clarinda reminded him when he grumped a little, but this was not what he had had in mind.

'This was not Rodin's side of Paris at all, was it?' she said. 'Or Gwen's.'

'They preferred the south side on the whole,' he agreed. 'The left bank.'

'That is where everything happens, isn't it? Where the artists live.'

'Not all. Colette lived on the right bank, beside the Palais Royale.' Clarinda had been telling him that she was reading the Claudine books. 'So did Cocteau, he was her neighbour,' he added, but Clarinda had not yet heard of him though he didn't doubt that she would, given time. And time, after all, was in her favour.

At the foot of Barbes, they came to a crossroads. He knew, since he had walked it before, that they should take the Boulevard de Magenta, a very long boulevard, indeed. This route march was beginning to seem to him quite ridiculous but he couldn't think what else to do but carry on.

*Was there nothing else you could have done, Mr Aherne? Did it not occur to you that Mr McCaffy and the other pupils might be worrying about you, wondering what had happened to you?*

He could possibly make a reverse charge call to the hotel but, first, he would have to get past the phlegmatic woman on the desk and then, if he did manage to speak to Alec, what could Alec do? Come in a taxi to fetch them? Alec was probably short of cash too.

Half way down Magenta, Clarinda had to stop. 'I think I've got a blister.' He had thought for the last while that she was walking in less sprightly fashion and was even limping a little but he had not thought it wise to comment on it. He knew, from his own daughter, how sensitive young girls were to any remarks that might remotely be considered critical. Clarinda unwound the thongs of her sandal from her ankle and took it off. Her heel looked horribly raw and inflamed.

'You should have said so before,' he said, touching her heel just above the sore part and shaking his head over it, forgetting that, as a teacher, he was not permitted to lay a finger on a pupil, whatever the circumstance. Her skin felt hot to his touch.

*Are you trying to tell us, Mr Aherne, that you did not lay a finger on this girl?*

'I don't suppose you've got any plasters on you?' said Cormac.

She shook her head. The plasters were also in Alec's little red knapsack. Cormac was beginning to feel annoyed that Alec had not waited for them. He had certainly not warmed to Alec McCaffy on this trip. He did not mind that he was ignorant about art, that had nothing to do with it. After all, he himself was not too hot where geography was concerned, he could still confuse the Arctic with the Antarctic, though geography did not seem to be much about that these days. A woman teacher was supposed to have come with him, to be a carer and mentor for the girls, but she had been summoned to hospital for an operation after waiting for nine months so she had not been able to turn down the offer. Alec had been the only teacher free enough of extra commitments to come with him.

'Well, now.' Cormac frowned at the wounded heel.

'I'll just have to go barefoot.'

She couldn't do that! The pavements were hard and the French didn't bother if their dogs fouled them, any more than the British did. Actually, less. Dodging dog turds was a daily hazard, they had found, and more than one student had managed to foul their trainers and carry with them a lingering smell of shit for the rest of the day. Clarinda took the sandals off, nevertheless.

They made it to the end of the boulevard and arrived at the windy Place de la Republique where they collapsed onto the ground. Clarinda's feet were grubby already.

'I don't mind,' she said, drawing up her knees and hugging them.

He had become aware that he was hungry, as well as thirsty. The sky was losing its colour fast and the street lights had come on when they were half way down the last boulevard. From here he was not sure what the most direct route would be down to the river and St Germain. He did not want to cross it too far east. When they had rested for a few minutes he got up and asked a passer-by and was directed to the rue du Temple, another long street but not so wide and exposed as the boulevards. He was definitely off boulevards. The air had cooled considerably in the last hour and Clarinda was wearing nothing on the upper part of her body but a skimpy shirt, not even a bra. Well, that was obvious; it wasn't that he was making an effort to look. He took off his sweatshirt and offered it to her.

She slipped it on. The shirt was too baggy and the sleeves too long but that only seemed to make her smile. She hugged her arms, wrapped in the overlong sleeves, around her. 'Thank you, Cormac,' she said.

Down the length of the rue du Temple they went, on his part wearily, though she stepped out as lightly as before, if more slowly. He had the feeling she was keeping pace with him in order not to tax him. When they sighted the towers of Notre Dame up ahead he wanted to cheer, instead of which he muttered, 'Thank God.' They crossed the river onto the left bank.

'I feel I've come home,' said Clarinda. 'This is definitely where I shall live when I come to Paris. Perhaps I shall even find a room in the rue du Cherche-Midi. Wouldn't it be a gas if I got one at number 87? And isn't a wonderful name - Cherche-Midi? Seek midday. Or the south. Which is it, Cormac?'

She was inclined to think he had the answer to everything about Paris, but he didn't. He had taken the name for what it was, the name of a street, without question. He supposed it could be either; both suggested warmth and sunshine. He had to tell her he did not know.

From the river it was still a good fifteen minute walk to their hotel. Alec was standing in the foyer, his feet apart, his knees braced, as if ready for some kind of action. He looked relieved at the sight of them, then he saw Clarinda's bleeding feet.

'Where on earth have you been?' he demanded.

# Chapter Eight

'The kids are talking, you know,' said Alec. He had tapped on Cormac's door and asked if he could come in for a nightcap. They had one together most nights. As well as having a drink they liked to recap on the day's events and discuss the next day's programme. Alex wasn't content unless everything was planned to the last detail. He feared disaster unless it was.

'Talking about what?' asked Cormac warily.

Alec was uncomfortable. 'You and Clarinda.'

'Me and Clarinda?' Cormac exploded. 'There's nothing to talk about.'

'You're always with her. Or she's always with you.' Alec corrected himself.

'So she was at my table at lunchtime. Effie McVeigh was at yours. You were talking to her twenty to the dozen.'

'About fault lines.'

'What do you think I was talking to Clarinda about?'

'I'm not suggesting you were talking to her about anything, well, *risky*.'

'Thank you for your confidence, Alec.'

'Now don't get annoyed with me. I just thought I should *warn* you. I'm sure there's nothing in it -'

'You're damned right there's nothing. You don't think that *I* -'

'Of course I don't. You wouldn't be so daft. Your job would be at stake. It's just that once talk starts ...' Alec cleared his throat and Cormac poured another splash of whisky into his glass and told him to drink up. 'Well, then, when you disappeared with her this afternoon -'

'We didn't *disappear*. We were looking for Cathy and Sue and you didn't wait for us. You had the bloody Métro tickets in your stupid backpack.'

Alec bridled. Cormac realised straightaway that he shouldn't have been so aggressive as to refer to the backpack as stupid since it would appear to be an integral part of Alec's being. He didn't feel like apologising, however.

Alec set his glass down on Cormac's bedside table and got up. 'I think you should be careful, Cormac. The girl appears to have the hots for you.'

'Says who?'

'Everybody.' Alec left the room.

*Mr McCaffy did warn you, didn't he, Mr Aberne, that it could be dangerous if you were to be seen associating too freely with one of the pupils?*

Cormac finished the whisky. He was not such a fool as to totally ignore McCaffy's warning though the man's use of the phrase 'the hots' made him want to slug him on Clarinda's behalf. Vulgar oaf that he was. He'd always thought there was something of the Uriah Heep in him with his clammy hands. Cormac knew that Clarinda liked being with him but that was because she enjoyed talking to him, was interested in what he had to say, and in the same things that he was. And maybe she was a little bit infatuated with him but kids had had crushes on teachers from time immemorial. Crushes were like bubbles; they blew up quickly and burst at the first sign of discouragement. He resolved to embark on a campaign of discouragement.

Next day, which was their last day in Paris, they broke into two groups: one, in the charge of Alec, was going back to the Pompidou Centre where they could enjoy the street theatre as well as the art; the other, led by Cormac, was heading out of Paris to Meudon to the Villa des Brilliants, the home of Rodin. The pupils had been allowed to choose, and most of them, predictably, had opted for the Pompidou; only a handful wanted to go on another Rodin outing. The handful consisted of Sue and Cathy, and Clarinda. Cormac was not sure why Cathy and Sue wanted to go but was glad that they did for it would not be considered seemly, he was sure, not in Alec's eyes, for him to go there with Clarinda and no chaperone, nor would he have wished it himself.

When he came down in the lift he found the three girls waiting for him in the foyer. Clarinda, who spoke passable French, was talking to the receptionist. She turned triumphantly to Cormac.

'I've found out what Cherche-Midi means! Seek the South! Madame says there's an astronomer's sign on the wall of number nineteen. That's how the street gets its name.'

She had to see it, of course - she was good at getting her way, he had come to realise, through sheer deter-mination - and so they progressed down the rue du Cherche-Midi and stopped outside number nineteen. There was the sign. Clarinda stood gazing at it and Cormac was able to hazard a guess at what was play-ing in her mind. *Gwen is standing here. She is looking at the sign and thinking of the warmth of the Midi. She is on her way home to her little room at number*

*eighty-seven where she will await the arrival of Rodin.*
*She will hear his heavy step on the stair, his broad*
*knuckles on the door, and her heart will flutter ...*

'Let's push on,' said Cormac, 'or we'll never get
there.'

He managed to manoeuvre himself between Sue and
Cathy, which meant that Clarinda had to walk on the
outside, by the kerb. Whenever they had to break ranks
to allow other people to pass he saw to it that they
reformed as before. Their journey out to Meudon
was not going to be straightforward, like the ride to
Clignancourt. They were on their way to the Métro at
Sêvres-Babylon. Clarinda was disappointed.

'Are we not going to take the train from Montparnasse?'
she asked. 'That was how Rodin usually went home.
And Gwen would see him to the station. Don't you
want to go the way Rodin went?'

'Not particularly,' said Cormac. 'And this is just as quick.
Probably quicker. It's a longer walk to Montparnasse.'

Clarinda should not object to a shorter walk. Her feet
must be in a mess after yesterday's boulevard hike
though she was not complaining. She never did, whereas the rest of them were always moaning about something, about having sore feet, being tired, hungry,
thirsty, too hot, or too cold. They would stop every
twenty minutes if allowed to take on cargo. Packets of
crisps, cans of coke, chocolate bars, anything that could
be put in the mouth. It was a wonder some of them
didn't carry dummies with them. And then of course
there were those who disappeared for a few minutes
every so often and came back reeking of cigarette
smoke. 'You must think I was born yesterday,' he told
them.

Today, Clarinda was wearing trainers and they all carried anoraks since rain was forecast. At Sèvres-Babylon they took the Métro line 12 to the terminus of Mairie d'Issy. He contrived to sit beside Cathy, which left Clarinda to sit with Sue behind them. If he wasn't careful they would be saying he was after Cathy! He could hear Clarinda telling Sue about Gwen John waiting for Rodin in the evening when he'd finished work at the studio.

'She was a kind of stalker, then?' said Cathy.

'I wouldn't call her that.'

'Yes, but to hang about waiting for him to throw her a few crumbs. Give us a break! Wouldn't catch me doing that for any guy.'

'She had been his mistress, don't forget.'

'Big deal. Then he dumped her, didn't he? Got what he wanted from her and said bye-bye, baby.'

'It was that ghastly American woman who was married to a French duke that messed it all up for her. She vamped him to bits and poor Gwen was left standing.'

'More fool her.'

'But she adored him.'

Cormac asked Cathy what she was going to do when she left school and set up a conversation for the two of them. She thought she might like to work for one of the building societies, which didn't seem to offer much scope for discussion though he struggled to engage in one. *Do you find the idea of mortgages interesting?* He could hardly ask her that though perhaps he should for she might. He was always interested in other people's interests. 'What draws you to that especially?' he asked. 'My dad works for the Woolwich,' she said.

159

'Gets me what you see in her,' Sue was saying to Clarinda. 'She sounds like a real drip.'

'I don't say I necessarily *admire* the way she carried on with Rodin. She did go over the top at times -'

'I'll say. Some of those letters, about her body yearning for his touch and wanting to put her lips against his neck, stuff like that. Could you imagine writing those things to a guy, especially one that doesn't want you?'

Clarinda murmured something, but whether she was agreeing or disagreeing it would have been difficult to say.

Sue went on, 'And then there was that bit about her setting light to her hair down *there* . I mean to say! And wanting to cut herself! She must have been bananas.'

'Only when she was desperate -'

'Is the Woolwich a good place to work?' asked Cormac but Cathy did not answer, she was too intent on listening to the conversation going on behind them. He wondered why Clarinda had been reading out bits of the diary to the girls when they would obviously not be sympathetic. She would have a hard job trying to convert them.

'But I do admire her work,' Clarinda was continuing. 'And, as a person, she intrigues me. That she could be so absolute. There is something about going to the edge -'

'Right, girls!' said Cormac, springing up.

They had reached the end of the line. They disembarked to find that the promised rain had arrived and was sheeting down. Cathy and Sue peered out into it, looking as if they would cut and run given the slightest encouragement.

'Anoraks on, hoods up!' said Cormac. They now had to catch a bus to Hôpital-Percy. After a fifteen minute wait at the stance, during which time Cathy and Sue groused about wet feet, a bus came, and a short ride took them to their destination.

The Villa des Brilliants was situated on a hill behind the military hospital looking down over the valley. The house was not brilliant, he had warned them, so that they would not be disappointed.

'It's kind of ugly,' said Cathy, as they approached it up a long drive. 'With that sticky-up grey slate roof and those wee dormer windows poking out. And I don't like red and white brick.'

'It's called the North Oxford style,' said Clarinda, before Cormac could respond. She had read it in a book, of course, one of the ones he had lent her. He was beginning to wonder if she knew them off by heart. 'It was the garden that Rodin liked so much. He loved sitting on a bench with his two dogs when it was getting dark, and watch the lights come on in Paris down below. Didn't he, Cormac?'

'I believe he did.'

'That's why he thought it worth the effort to walk to the station at Montparnasse every night and make the journey out here. It would be wonderful to work out here. Wouldn't it, Cormac?' Clarinda's eyes had that shiny look again.

'I guess it would,' he said. When he had first come he had had the same thought, had imagined himself working in the pavilion where many of Rodin's rough casts were on display.

'Once, when Rodin was away,' said Clarinda, 'Gwen brought her cat and camped in the bushes and sketched the house. Rose Beuret, that's the old peasant woman he lived with, came out into the garden and pottered about with the two dogs but she didn't see Gwen. Lucky the dogs didn't smell the cat! Gwen wasn't jealous of Rose, though. She felt that Rose kept Rodin's other women away.' Clarinda laughed. 'But can't you just imagine it - Gwen crouching in the bushes there trying to keep her cat quiet!'

'What was she doing bringing her cat with her?' asked Sue.

'She adored her cats. She liked to paint them. On the way home in the tram the cat shot out the door when it stopped at St Cloud and Gwen nearly went off her head. She leapt off the tram herself but there was no sign of Tiger- that was the cat's name. She spent nine days living rough on a piece of waste ground near the river looking for him. But she did find him in the end.'

'I think she was off her head anyway,' said Cathy.

She was an artist,' said Clarinda, going ahead.

'Are all artists potty?' asked Cathy.

'Most of them are fairly neurotic,' said Cormac. 'They possibly have to be in order to persevere.' Though as he said this he wondered if Rodin could be called neurotic. He'd been obsessed by his work. But was that the same thing? He'd always had an image of the sculptor as a man securely earthed, with a strong centre and a deep religious but not fanatical faith.

They paid their entrance money and went into the house. It was quite modest, having only three bedrooms upstairs, which they were not permitted to see, and on the ground floor, a dining room, a small salon and Rodin's *atelier*, all of which were open for inspection.

The interior, however, was light, with its long windows and attractive avocado-green and cream decor. The dining room was the part of the house they found most *sympathique*. They lingered there, imagining Rodin seated at the table, served by the elderly peasant woman. Even Cathy liked the room.

'It must have been peaceful for him to come back to after the hurly-burly of Paris,' said Cormac. 'Here, he could relax. Rose appears to have been undemanding.' He was thinking that perhaps all artists could do with a Rose but would not have dared say so. He would have been torn limb from limb by Cathy and Sue, metaphorically speaking, of course.

'The women in Paris that mobbed him seemed to have been demanding enough.' Cathy shook her head. 'I still don't understand how he managed to pull them all so easily. I mean, I know he was a genius but he was no looker. And he was *old*. Same age as my granda.'

'One night,' said Clarinda, in the voice of a story-teller, 'Gwen followed him home.'

'Not for the first time, I bet,' interrupted Cathy.

'She crept up the garden to that window there and looked in on him and Rose and watched them at their meal.'

'She was lucky she wasn't arrested,' said Cathy.

'You could go on that Mastermind, Clarinda,' said Sue, 'and answer questions on Gwen John.'

Clarinda had not heard. She had gone to stand in the doorway of Rodin's *atelier* with a rapt look on her face.

The sun emerged as they came out of the house. They went next to the pavilion in the garden, which had been erected after Rodin's death. On entering it, Clarinda gasped. The long building was filled with white plaster casts of his sculptures and terracotta models, the whole lit by golden sunshine.

'I didn't expect all this,' she said happily. 'To see so many together, and with this light!' The room was quiet, and uncrowded, unlike the museum in Paris. There were only two other visitors apart from themselves and they were soon to depart.

Cathy and Sue did a quick tour round and said they'd wait for them outside.

Cormac and Clarinda moved slowly round the room, stopping for long spells in time in front of each exhibit. There were studies and casts for many of his major works which, as Cormac pointed out, gave an insight into the artist's method of working.

'He was so wonderful with clothes, wasn't he?' said Clarinda, when they came to the statue of one, Bastien-Lépage. 'Look at the creases in those boots, they look like real leather, and the breeches! You want to touch them to see if they're made of real material.' She was breathless with admiration.

'He was a genius,' said Cormac.

They came to a cast of *The Kiss*.

'It's beautiful,' whispered Clarinda, 'even as a plaster cast.'

He felt a tightening in his throat.

'Cormac,' she said, looking up into his face.

'We must go,' he said. 'Sue and Cathy are waiting.'

'Please! I've got to tell you. I've fallen in love with you.'

'No, you have not, Clarinda. ' He spoke gently. 'You're just carried away by visions of Gwen John.'

She shook her head. She appeared to be calmer than he felt. 'You're wrong. And it doesn't matter what you say, it won't change how I feel.'

'Hey, you two!' called Cathy from the doorway. 'Will you be long? Sue and I thought we might go and see if we can find a cafe.'

'No,' said Cormac, 'wait for us in the garden! We're just coming!'

By the time Clarinda accedes to his request to leave the shop and get out of his way Cormac realises he is going to be late for Davy. He stashes the bucket in the corner and flings down the mop. He'll come in tomorrow morning, Saturday, when he doesn't open the shop, and do the rest of the clearing up.

As he is putting on his jacket in the back shop he hears the door open. Surely she's not come back! He goes through to the front. The girl closing the door is not Clarinda, but his own daughter.

'Oh, it's you, Sophie.'

'Who did you think it was?'

'You're out of school early.'

She says she hasn't been in today, she wasn't feeling well in the morning. She looks well enough to him but he doesn't want an argument so he doesn't say so. He feels half the time that he is being blackmailed by his children.

'You wouldn't have any sandwiches left, would you?'

'There's a couple in the fridge but listen, Sophie, I'm in a hurry. I'm late for Davy.'

'It won't take a minute.'

There are three cling-filmed wrapped sandwiches on focaccia bread, marked mozzarella, tomato and basil. She drops them into her bag. 'Could I have a couple of bags of crisps?' She throws in four and two cans of Fanta.

'Sophie, be quick!' says Cormac.

'All right, all right, I'm coming.'

'Who are you planning to feed? The five thousand?'

'I'll see you tomorrow,' she says and skips out of the door in front of him.

He arrives at the school to find Davy standing by the gate gazing up the street with the face of an abandoned child. The playground behind him is empty.

'Sorry, Davy old son!'

'I thought you weren't coming. Everybody else is gone.' The boy is close to tears. Cormac puts an arm round him but is shrugged off.

'You know I'd always come, you should never doubt that. I got held up. A couple of late customers.'

'Can I go to Mum's tonight?'

Cormac sighs. *Oh yes, go ahead and punish me! Everybody else is keen to so why not you?* His spirits, which were not that elevated to start with, fall even lower. This is one of those days when the gods are showering down every kind of rubbish they can find on top of his head.

'Can I?' Davy asks again.

'I'll ring her when she gets in from work.'

Davy cheers up, which does not cheer his father who, until recent times, has thought himself a pretty good father who loves his children and enjoys them and makes time for them and is loved by his children in return. Now it seems that Davy can't wait to get away from him.

He rings Rachel's number at six and gets the answering machine. He rings at seven and gets it again. And at eight. It is not worth trying after that. It is time for Davy to go to bed.

166

'You'll be seeing her tomorrow, anyway,' says Cormac as he makes hot chocolate for his son and sets out a chocolate biscuit on a plate beside it. Bribery and corruption. After Davy has gone to bed and been read to for fully twenty-five minutes he washes the dishes and loads up the washing machine. Then, at ten, he presses the redial button on the phone once more.

Sophie answers. She sounds short of breath.

'Have you just come in?'

'No.' She is lying, he can hear it in her voice. He is not as foolish as Mrs Bain as to think his daughter always tells the truth. He thinks too much still about Mrs Bain, which is not good for his blood pressure. He sees her satin arm with its shimmering dragons lifting the receiver and hears her plum-filled voice saying, 'Officer, I'd like to make a complaint.'

'I've been in a while,' his daughter is saying.

'So what did you do with yourself this afternoon?'

'Went to Tilda's.'

'Was she not at school either?'

'After she came back.'

'And before?'

'I just wandered about.'

As lonely as a cloud. Not lonely at all, he'd lay a bet on that.

'I'm in the middle of my homework,' she says.

'I'd better not keep you then. Is your mother there?'

'No, she's not back yet.'

'It's not her badminton night, is it?'

Sophie's response is defensive. 'I've no idea.' Is she protecting her mother? She doesn't have to of course: Rachel is free to do what she wants. *What is she doing? And with whom?*

167

'See you tomorrow then.'

He is determined, this weekend, to be firm with Sophie. Lay down the law.

'You *must* come back tonight,' he tells her. 'I don't want any of this staying at Tilda's lark, and you're to be in by eleven-thirty.'

'*Half-eleven*? None of my friends are home before two.'

'Twelve then. And I want to know where you're going and who you're going with and if you're not here by midnight I'll come and fetch you. *Comprendido*?'

'All right! You don't have to shout.'

She goes out mid-afternoon, but not before leaving an address. Cormac watches Saturday sport on the telly, then makes an omelette which he consumes with the best part of a bottle of red wine. He has a free evening ahead and doesn't know what to do with it. The trouble is most of his male friends are married and have their Saturday nights spoken for. Everybody loves Saturday night! Not if you're on your tod you don't. You feel you should be doing something other than lounge around. He decides to give Ken Mason a ring on the off chance that he might free for a drink. Ken says there's nothing he'd have liked better but they are committed elsewhere.

'Remember April, that woman you were speaking to at our party? She's giving a dinner. She's found herself a new man, a lawyer, widower, plenty of money. She wants to show him off.'

'Have a good time,' says Cormac, putting down the receiver.

He goes along to a pub in St Stephen's Street for a

while but nearly everyone looks under twenty-five, and he is wary of bumping into Clarinda again. Edinburgh is a small place if you want to avoid someone. Too small for him, with hundreds of his ex-pupils milling about, knowing too much about him. There are a couple in the pub but he doesn't think they've noticed him. They're not coming over to slap him on the back, at any rate, and say nice to see you. Nor are they glancing covertly in his direction and whispering behind their hands. Maybe he should go to Dublin, make a fresh start, and insist on taking Davy with him. But what kind of a life would it be for the boy waiting in the upstairs' flat for his father to come up at midnight reeking of cigarette smoke and beer from the bar?

Coming back through Stockbridge, preoccupied with such unproductive thoughts, he bumps into Archie Gibson, his former headmaster and friend. He still regards Archie as a friend but they've fallen out of the habit of seeing each other. After his suspension it was too difficult.

Archie is about to go into a restaurant with two people, a man and a woman, neither of whom Cormac recognises.

'Archie, hi there!'

'Oh hello, Cormac. How are you?' Archie is more embarrassed than he is; his time in the wilderness taught him to grow a thicker skin. Archie's friends go ahead into the restaurant.

'I'm not bad,' says Cormac. 'Surviving, at any rate.'

'Good. That's great. I've been meaning to give you a call.'

'I've moved.'

'Yes, I heard.'

'Sheila not with you?'

'No, no she's not.' Archie clears his throat, finishing with a cough. He looks away. 'Actually, we're not together any more.'

'Oh, I'm sorry. I hadn't heard.'

'These things happen.'

'Too true.' Cormac warms to the idea of renewing the friendship, now that they are in the same boat, in one respect, anyway. 'Let's have a drink one night, OK? I'll give you a call."

'Fine, fine.' Archie glances through the restaurant window.

'You'd better go,' says Cormac.

'Yes.' Archie's throat is bothering him again. 'It was most unfortunate, all that business.'

'It was.'

Cormac leaves Archie and walks through to the Colonies, reflecting on Archie's nervousness. He's been left with the feeling that Archie would just as soon he didn't bother to call. Maybe he's just thrown by the break-up of his own marriage. He and Rachel used to think Archie and his wife were not a well-matched pair: she liked the glamorous life, cruises, expensive hotels; he liked hill walking and camping in the Cevennes. But they had agreed that one could never tell looking in on a marriage from the outside.

So Cormac goes home to watch Saturday night telly, which proves to be dire, and is half asleep when he hears the key grate in the lock and Sophie say, 'It's me, Dad.'

He looks at his watch. It is twenty to one, which is not bad, and he won't even mention she's late. This is what he'd call within bounds. It's as well she has come in; he wouldn't be in much of state to cycle over to Mandy's on the other side of town.

She has a mark under her right eye. He puts up his hand to touch the side of her face and she backs away. He frowns.

'Is that bruise a you've got there?'

'I bumped into a door.'

It sounds like a stock excuse, the first to come to mind. He pushes it no further but he's bothered. He can't show it of course as that would only cause more irritation on her part. She easily becomes irritable these days.

He makes hot chocolate for them both and they sit talking till two, which cheers him. He has always felt close to his daughter, until the last few months. She is talking about going to drama school; she'd like to be a director or producer, not an actor. She is producing the school play with another girl.

*Romeo and Juliet*: more star-crossed lovers, like Paolo and Francesca. Them! The crossing of stars appeals to Sophie. She loves Shakespeare. She loves *Romeo and Juliet*.

'You must come, Dad.'

'Oh, I will. I wouldn't miss it for the world.'

He goes to bed feeling happier than he has done since he and Rachel took the decision to split. They agonised over it for weeks but, in the end, when they did decide, it seemed inevitable. And it still does.

In the morning, waking later than usual, he gets up to find a note on the kitchen table.

'Gone out to meet Tilda. Back for lunch at Mum's. Sophie xx.'

Fair enough. He doesn't expect her to sit in on a

Sunday morning and keep him company though he was going to suggest they went for a walk in the Botanic Garden. She used to love doing that with him when she was small. But she is no longer small and she doesn't consider an outing to feed the ducks exciting. He longs to know what does excite her. He goes upstairs whistling to make the bed and tidy Davy's room for his return that evening. He always complains loudly if Sophie has messed up his stuff. He's a tidy boy, takes after him in that respect rather than his mother. Surprisingly, Rachel is not very tidy, except in her person, whereas he likes order and hates random mess. People knowing them, though not intimately, would imagine that their penchants for tidiness would operate the other way round. His studio might have looked messy to the casual viewer but everything in it was in a state of transformation, of being processed into some form of order.

As he is plumping up the downie he notices a bag sticking from from under the bed. Sophie always leaves something behind. He pulls the bag out. It is a manky old sports holdall and should be thrown out. She doesn't have to cart a thing like that about! They're not that hard up, even though he is only earning tiddlywinks so far with his sandwiches. The rent and council tax are crippling and he has to pay off the loan on his equipment before he can go into the black.

He looks at the bag. The zip has stuck on some cloth half way along, showing signs of having been pulled together hastily or, if he knows Sophie, impatiently. It is his excuse to open the bag: to release the trapped cloth in case it might be an important piece of clothing. Otherwise, he wouldn't have touched it; he regards other people's property as sacred, including his children's, and not to be tampered with. Unless one suspects them of something. Does he suspect Sophie? Of course he does. And of course he is curious, as well as a little apprehensive, to find out what is in the bag. Drugs? Every parent's nightmare: to open a bag and find something nasty lurking in the bottom.

With a tug the zip comes unstuck and he pulls out a pair of holey jeans, extremely holey jeans. Being caught in a zip wouldn't affect their condition much. He knows there's a trend from time to time for the young to wear jeans with holes in the knee and let the wind whistle through to chap their skin, but this is surely going beyond the boundaries of fashion. And they're filthy. Bogging, they would have called them back home. So, too, is an old sweatshirt of an indecipherable colour, and as for the pair of trainers! Aren't kids supposed to be fussy about what they wear on their feet? Nike or nothing. Not his daughter, obviously. These trainers are worse than anything Davy has ever had even after weeks of ball-kicking and kerb-scraping. And the whole lot stinks.

But there is no alcohol in the bag, or cigarettes, or drugs. That's a relief. He puts everything back into the bag and shoves it under the bed with his toe and then goes and washes the smell off his hands. Sophie used to be so fussy about cleanliness; she sometimes had two baths a day, using up all the hot water. But she must have been wearing these clothes or else what was she doing with them?

After lunch he mentions it to Rachel. Sophie has taken Davy out to Inverleith Park to play football. They were both getting restless.

'I don't know what clothes you're talking about, Cormac.' Rachel frowns.

'In an old blue sports bag.'

Rachel shakes her head. 'Sophie doesn't have a blue sports bag. I'll take a look later when she brings her stuff back. But you know she won't listen to me when it comes to what clothes she should wear!'

They discuss their children. Rachel thinks they're not behaving much differently from how they were before, certainly not Sophie. 'She's totally wrapped up in her own affairs. It's the age.'

'Bloody awful age. Pity they can't go to sleep and wake up when they're eighteen.'

They hear the children laughing as they come up the outside stair. They arrive with glowing faces, and licking ice cream cones, which Sophie has bought. They met Sophie's friend Tilda in the park, they say.

'Tilda can't kick for toffee,' says Davy.

'I'm not a bad kicker, though, am I, Davy?' Sophie gives him a dig in the ribs. 'Go on, admit it! I gave you a good run for your money.'

Cormac and Rachel smile at each other, reassured, so that when Cormac returns home to find his Aunt Mary on the line within minutes of his opening the door, his spirits do not do their customary nose-dive.

'How're you doing, Aunt Mary? We're doing great here. The kids are fine. I'm fine. Rachel's fine. Sends her love to you all.' Rachel has never been able to stomach Mary, the aunt of the sly remarks. *Of course you won't have time to make soup for your children, will you? Or iron their clothes. Or see to their souls.* A heathen for a mother! And out all day, never in the house when she's needed. Healing the sick, Cormac would remind her, but Aunt Mary doesn't see why that shouldn't be left to men.

'Nice talking to you, Aunt Mary,' says Cormac, managing to terminate the call before she embarks on what a poor son he is to his mother.

'I think we'll take Sophie over to Belfast with us when we go at Easter,' he says to Davy. 'We could have good fun, the three of us. We can go down to Bangor and kick a ball on the sands.'

'She won't want to come. She says she's going away at Easter.'

'Oh, she does, does she?' The feeling of reassurance hasn't lasted long. 'Did she say where?' If she thinks she's going to Greece she can think again.

Davy shrugs.

'Has she a boyfriend, do you know?' Cormac disapproves of pumping one child to find out information about another. There's nothing like having children for throwing all your principles out the window.

'She knows lots of boys.'

'I'm sure. But has she a steady boyfriend?'

'She's in love. I heard her telling Tilda when we were at the park.'

In love. That could mean all manner of things. It doesn't necessarily mean she has a steady boyfriend. She could have a crush on her English teacher. That idea gives him pause for a further thought: it might be why she has suddenly become so enthusiastic about Shakespeare.

# Chapter Nine

It was their last night in Paris and Cormac was packing his bag ready for an early departure in the morning. He was not having a nightcap with Alec this evening. Alec had said good night when they'd got out of the lift. He'd said it stiffly, adding, 'I'll see you in the morning.' He was not a man to forgive slights easily.

Cormac was surprised, then, when there came a tap on his door. Perhaps he had misjudged poor McCaffy. In a rush of *bonhomie* he opened the door wide, prepared to invite him in to share the last of the whisky.

'Can I come in?' asked Clarinda.

He half closed the door. 'You certainly cannot! For God's sake, Clarinda, what do you think you're doing to me?' The walls of the hotel were thin, and behind every wall on this floor there were students, one or two of whom might be asleep; but the majority could be counted on to be wide awake knocking back smuggled cans of beer and bottles of wine, having a party for their last night in Paris. He had seen the bulging carrier bags being carried in and had turned a blind eye, on the understanding that there were to be no drugs. He had delivered a stern lecture on that.

'Please, Cormac,' pleaded Clarinda. 'I just want to be with you, to talk to you.'

'Well, I don't want to talk to you! So, for Christ's sake scram!'

She burst into tears. 'You don't have to be so horrible to me,' she cried and ran along the corridor, making for the staircase, by-passing the lift.

He swore and sat down on the edge of the bed to put on his socks and shoes, then he went after her. He took the lift and when he emerged he found the front lobby empty, except for the night porter, who was watching a small television set. Had he seen a girl, one of the students? asked Cormac. The man certainly had. The young woman had been very distressed; he'd tried to stop her, but she'd opened the door and run out into the street. Had he seen which way she went? He shrugged. *Merci,* said Cormac, and went out into the street himself.

He stood on the pavement and examined the street to the right and to the left. There was no sign of her, of anyone. The French were not late-bedders, even the Parisians; they often ate as early as the British. It was Sunday night, too, and more than half the restaurants had been closed. They'd found a large boulevard brasserie to eat in, down on St Germain. He had sat at a different table to Clarinda and and had made a point of not looking in her direction. She had been very quiet and eaten very little, which had been noticed by Alec, who had commented on it to Cormac afterwards and wondered if she was feeling all right. 'Was she OK when she was with you at Meudon?'

A slight drizzle was falling, leaving drops of pearly moisture on the car rooftops. He had come out in his shirt. *Tant pis.* Where the hell had she gone? 'Clarinda!' he called tentatively, expecting no response and getting none. This damn fool girl was making him sweat. He wished Rachel were here; she would know how to handle it. He might ring her when he got back to his room and talk it over with her. She had had to cope with most human conditions in her surgery.

He went to the corner of the street where it ran into the rue du Cherche-Midi. It was remarkably quiet and still. A cat was yowling but that was about all. He began to walk in the direction of number 87. The room Gwen John had rented there had been her favourite of all the ones she had inhabited around Paris. In his mind's eye he saw a room barely furnished with a wicker chair and a simple table on which rests a bowl of soft yellow primroses. The window, screened with white muslin, lets light into the room. She painted it at dawn, for Rodin. She told him she had awakened to see the room in a different, almost mysterious light, and wanted him to see it too. How strange, thought Cormac, as he stood on the corner, that such a serene painting came from such a troubled soul. How odd, too, that he should have such a strong vision of that dawn painting when he was abroad on this dark night devoured by anxiety for the wellbeing of Clarinda Bain. He had thought Clarinda mature for her age and better balanced than many of the pupils; now she was acting like a child. He knew that was often how it was in the teenage years, with mood changes swinging wildly between two poles, but knowing it did not console him. He realised that he did not know what Clarinda was capable of. Throwing herself into the Seine? Surely not. Though he felt sure that Gwen John must have contemplated suicide.

As he neared number 87 he had a strong sensation that Clarinda - and the ghost of Gwen John - would be somewhere around here, hovering in the shadows, holding their breath, waiting for him to follow. He stood still to listen, trying not to move a muscle, as if he were playing the game of statues. Was it a game Clarinda was playing with him? A cat, perhaps the one that been yowling, ran out from under one of the parked cars. He began to walk again, very slowly, making as little noise as possible.

He had taken only a few steps when she moved. She came out of the shadows of a doorway on the opposite pavement and flew off on winged feet up the street. She took off so quickly and quietly that she surprised him and he lost a few seconds while he gathered himself together. She had a good start on him yet he did not doubt that she would want to be caught, at some point. If his heart would hold out until then! He could feel it pumping away under his damp shirt. He was glad of the cooling mizzle of rain on his overheated head. He could hear nothing but the thud of his own footsteps on the pavement and the harsh flow of his breath. He kept his eyes focused on the dark moving figure ahead.

She turned left at the end of Cherche-Midi onto the Boulevard Montparnasse. He redoubled his effort now that she was out of sight. When he reached the corner he could see no sign of her on the boulevard. There were a few people about but no one was running. He stopped there on the corner and let his heart subside for a moment. God damn her! She could be hiding in the shadow of another doorway, watching for him; or she might have crossed the road to go up the avenue du Maine. He had a sudden thought. She might be heading for the Montparnasse station, silly little fool that she was.

He waited for two cars and a motor scooter to pass, then he sprinted across the broad street and a few yards along branched into the avenue du Maine. He still had no sighting of her but he pressed on, pushing himself as hard as he dared. The station was not far, especially when one was running. Then he saw her: she was leaning against the station wall, her back flat against it as if she were awaiting execution, or a proposition. A nearby light illuminated her face, showing up its planes and angles. She had good bone structure, would age well. He could imagine making a head of her though knew he would not.

He jogged up to her and confronted her, his hands on his hips, allowing his breathing to settle back into a normal rhythm.

'Clarinda,' he said wearily. Didn't she realise she could be taken for a prostitute standing there? Didn't she realise how provocative she looked and how dangerous was her mood?

'Cormac,' she said, shifting her position slightly, letting her shoulders droop.

'You gave me a hell of a fright,' he said, putting his hands her shoulders. 'Running off like that.' She was trembling and her long eyelashes glinted with teardrops.

'Why do you hate me?' she asked in a small voice.

'I don't hate you. It's just that what you want from me is impossible.'

'Nothing is impossible, if you want it enough.'

He has said that himself, more than once, but not for a long time.

She moved out from the wall and into his arms and her face turned up to his and the next thing that he knew was that his hot dry mouth had met her soft young one and was drawing in its sweetness. They were locked in a kiss.

Back at the hotel, Emma, Clarinda's room-mate, awoke at two am - she had not gone to any of the parties on account of a headache - to find the other bed empty. 'Clarinda?' she called. She got up and looked in the bathroom but it, too, was empty. She pulled on jeans and a sweatshirt and padded along the corridor and knocked on Cormac's door. When there was no response she went on to Alec's room and knocked there. He came to the door in red and white striped pyjamas with his hair sticking up at the back. He blinked at Emma.

'What's up?'

'I can't find Clarinda.'

'Can't *find* her?' It took a minute or two for Alec to realise what the girl was talking about but then he wasted no time. He pulled on his dressing gown and with Emma following on behind he went striding along to Cormac's room.

'I've already knocked,' said Emma. 'He must be fast asleep.'

Alec knocked firmly and insistently and pursed his lips when nothing happened. He told Emma to run along back to bed and not to worry, then he descended in the lift to the lobby. The night porter was watching a black and white film on his television set. Alec recognised Humphrey Bogart.

'*Excusez-moi*,' he began.

The porter looked round.

'Have you see one of the pupils?' asked Alec in

English. '*Elevès. Ouì? Et Monsieur Aherne? L'homme.*'
He tapped himself on the chest. '*Comme moi.*'

'*Mais, ouì!*' The porter pointed to the door.

Gone out?' asked Alec. '*Sortis?*'

'*Oui, ils sont sortis.*'

Alec went to the glass door and stood with crossed arms gazing out into the dark, wet street. He turned, hearing a noise behind him and saw Emma coming out of the lift with Cathy and Sue.

'We heard Clarinda was missing,' said Cathy. 'We're dead worried about her so we wondered if there was anything we could do.'

'There's nothing,' said Alec sharply. 'You'd do better to go and get some sleep. We have an early start in the morning.'

'Emma thinks Cormac might be missing too,' said Sue in a voice that was intended to sound innocent.

'Perhaps they've eloped,' said Cathy and then all three girls broke into giggles.

Cormac and Clarinda drew back from their kiss. He now was the one who was trembling. *Ae fond kiss...* The line ran through his head bringing with it the terrifying thought of Mrs Bain.

'Clarinda,' he breathed, shaking his head. *Ae fond kiss, and then we sever.* There would be no option but to sever and it must be done quickly.

'Cormac,' she said softly, putting up her hand to touch his face. He caught hold of the her fingers and trapped them.

'Listen, Clarinda -' He could scarcely get past her name. She was looking up at him, her eyes luminous in the lamplight. 'I'm sorry, I truly am. It shouldn't have happened.'

'What - the *kiss*? Of course it should. It had to! It was destined to, don't you see?'

'I want you to forget that it ever did.'

'How can I forget something like that? Can you?'

'We've got to. It was a moment of madness.'

'I love being mad! I'm glad it happened. Aren't you glad, Cormac? You liked it, didn't you? You know you did. You didn't pull away from me. You wanted it!'

She wanted him to kiss her again, he was aware of that, how could he not when the signals were so obvious? He was aware also that she was determined to try to make it happen. He felt unnerved by her straightforwardness. She was young, and although not a total innocent abroad she was still able to believe that if you wanted something badly enough you should go for it and to hang with the consequences.

And he wanted to kiss her again, which was unnerving him even more. She was sweet and young and refreshing and, in the middle of the kiss, which had lasted he knew not how long, whether it had been seconds or minutes, he had felt young again himself, freed of all the shackles that bound him. How seductive that was! For that brief spell of time he had felt anything might be possible. But he was not as naive as she was and now that he had drawn back he faced anew what he had known since he was a child: that you could not always have what you wanted, or, if you did, the price to pay would be much too high.

'I'm your teacher, Clarinda.' He took hold of her wrists; she was trying to close in on him again. 'I am here in *loco parentis*.'

'My mother wouldn't mind. She thinks love is the

most important thing in life. She says without it the world is grey. She's very romantic.'

'You haven't discussed me with your mother?' The idea alarmed him.

'Not exactly. Not *discussed*. But she knows I admire you. She does, too. She loved your exhibition when I brought her in the summer. She'd have bought your flamingo if she could have afforded it.'

Fleetingly he felt some warmth towards Mrs Bain. The flamingo had been one of his favourite pieces. It had been bought by Rachel's father, which had embarrassed him for he had felt that his father-in-law was probably doing it in order to encourage him and give their family finances a little pep-up. Two other pieces had been bought by friends of his mother-in-law. He said, 'I don't know whether your mother would mind or not, Clarinda, but plenty of other people would, including my wife, whom I love. She is not a Rose Beuret. And apart from all that, I could get into very serious trouble.'

'How could you? Only you and I know' She smiled at him, with the smile of a woman light years older. 'Only you and I need to know.'


'What are you up to these days, Sophie?' he asks his daughter as they sit drinking a late-night cup of hot chocolate together. It is actually two o'clock in the morning and she has not long come in. She has been back-sliding and it will soon be time for him to read another riot act and lay down the rules yet again. With Sophie it is very much a case of giving her the inch with the full knowledge that she will take much more than a mile. He has sat waiting for her, dozing a little, then jerking awake to go out and stand on the top step gazing up the street, listening to the snarl of the wind as it prowled down the terrace. When he heard the hee-haw of a police siren his immediate thought was that it might be Sophie who was in trouble. Since becoming a single parent his anxiety level has risen distinctly.

He asks his question as if he is not at all bothered about what Sophie is up to but, of course, he knows and she knows, that he is.

'Nothing much,' she says, cradling her cup between her hands, which look rather grubby. Her long hair falls like a curtain on either side of her face so that he cannot see her expression. She is wearing a bulky greenish-khaki garment which could be either clean or dirty. His nose twitches. She has that mouldy smell again.

'Where do you go? Discos?' Surely not, looking like that! But how would he know?

'I wish you wouldn't cross-question me all the time.'

'I don't, not all the time. I restrain myself often, believe me! But I have a right to ask where you go until this time in the morning. You're under age and in my care and I do care what happens to you. I don't expect you to tell me *all* the details but I'd like to feel you could talk to me, like a pal of sorts, tell me what's going on in your head. Your life!' he ends, mock-dramatically, so that she won't think he's being too heavy. He often knows that he shouldn't press on when he does. He is sure Rachel is much more subtle when she pumps the children for information, and more successful.

'You don't tell me what's going on in your life,' says Sophie. 'You didn't tell me about Clarinda.'

She has got the knife in between his ribs now. He wants to fold over, and nurse his wounds. When they told her about his suspension from school and the charge being made against him they had gone into few details and she had asked few questions. And as far as Cormac knows, they managed to keep it from Davy. But kids have a way of finding out things and understanding more than you give them credit for.

'You don't know Clarinda, do you?' he asks, appalled that she might.

'No, but my friend Tilda does. She says Clarinda was madly in love with you.'

'But I am, Cormac,' said Clarinda. 'I can't help it. Why don't you believe me?'

'Of course you can help it.' He spoke gently to her. 'You talked yourself into it in the first place. It's just a notion you've got.'

'That's not true!' She started to cry, which gave him no option but to put his arms round her and comfort her. She was small and soft against him and her hair smelt of fresh rain. He felt her lips against his neck and a shiver ran up his spine making his shoulders twitch. For a moment he was tempted to bury his face in her hair and forget the world, Alec McCaffy, and all the rest of them. Instead he eased her firmly away from him again and held her at arm's length.

'Now listen to me, Clarinda. It'll pass, believe me it will. After you've been home for a week you'll laugh about all this.'

'You can't stop me loving you.'

'You're not Gwen John,' he told her. 'And I'm not Rodin.'

187

'He was often horrible to her but that didn't stop her loving him. And it didn't stop him making love to her.'

'We must go.' His chest felt tight. 'Come on!'

'She wouldn't move.

'All right, suit yourself, stay there,' he said, using the tone of voice he might to his daughter when his patience was running out.

He turned away from her but after the first dozen or so steps he was forced to look round. She was leaning against the wall again looking like a floppy doll. A man had stopped on the pavement and was looking at her.

Cormac walked back.

'Clarinda, now you are behaving like a three-year-old!'

'I want you to make love to me.'


'Clarinda talked a lot of nonsense,' he says to his daughter. 'Her mother filled her head with romantic tosh. She was in love with Burns! Her mother, that is.'

'What's wrong with Burns?'

'Nothing. Not his poetry, anyway. But Mrs Bain was in love with the man, or her idea of the man. Clarinda told me she kept a picture of him on her bedside table as well as on the piano.' He had seen the one on the piano, on the only occasion that he visited the Bains' flat.

'You had a mega-sized blown-up photo of Rodin on the wall of your studio. You said it inspired you. You said you felt he was watching over you and telling you to hang in there. What's the difference? Maybe the picture of Burns was inspiring her to write poetry.'

'But I wasn't in love with Rodin. Mrs Bain recites a Burns poem before she goes to sleep at night. Instead of a prayer, I suppose. *My love is like a red, red rose. Trouble is roses have thorns.*' He speaks jocularly in an effort to lighten the topic but his daughter is in a dogged mood, determined not to let him off the hook.

'So it was all her mother's fault? Because she had a picture of Burns on her bedside table?'

'I didn't say that. I'm just saying that Tilda should not believe everything that Clarinda tells her. But we've wandered rather far away from you. Are *you* in love with anyone? Or wouldn't you tell me if you were?' He tries to smile.

Sophie shrugs and tilts her mug to drain the last drops of her chocolate drink. She runs the tip of her tongue round her lips.

'So which is it?' He keeps the teasing voice. 'You won't tell me?'

'You wouldn't approve of him,' she says and goes into the kitchen to rinse her mug under the tap.

Eventually he managed to prise Clarinda away from the wall and coax her to come with him. She dragged her feet every step of the way. She was back to being a child again. A petulant, spoiled, sulking child, who could not get her way. His patience was spent and with it had gone his desire for her. He was wet, exhausted, and irritable. He remembered suddenly that he had a fifty franc note in his trouser pocket which he had put there earlier as an emergency back-up. He'd been determined not to be caught out as he had been coming back from the flea market.

'I'm going to try and get a taxi,' he said, bringing Clarinda to a halt on the edge of the kerb.

'I want to walk. And I don't want to go back to the hotel.'

A taxi was approaching. He stepped out into the road raising his hand. The car pulled up with a squeal of tires.

Clarinda had retreated into a doorway.

'*Un moment, s'il vous plait,*' said Cormac through the taxi window.

*Jeune, eh?* said the driver, looking past him at Clarinda.

Cormac felt like a dirty old man. He went over to Clarinda and pleaded with her in a low voice. He felt like threatening to abandon her altogether, except that that would offer further opportunities for drama. Was it what she wanted, to be the centre of a drama? It was not the time to try and fathom Clarinda's motives.

'If you carry on like this any more you'll make me hate you, Clarinda!'

'Don't be so angry with me!' She was going to cry again.

'Then, come!'

She let him lead her to the cab and bundle her into the back seat. She leant against him as they swung hectically through the quiet streets. Cormac was aware of the driver watching them in his mirror, the thin line of his moustache curled into a little smile of amusement.

As they reached their destination the door of the hotel swung open and out stepped Alec McCaffy in his red and white striped pyjamas and blue Paisley-patterned dressing gown. He waited on the pavement while Cormac paid off the driver and handed Clarinda out of the back of the cab.

'*Bonne nuit,*' said the driver in a voice that made Cormac want to push in his *louche* face.

Alec held the hotel door open for Clarinda. 'I suggest you go straight to bed, Clarinda.' He let the door swing shut and then he turned to face Cormac. 'What has been going on, Aherne?'

'Nothing, Mr McCaffy. Nothing of the sort that you are imagining. Clarinda became hysterical and ran off so I had no option but to go out and bring her back. You would have had to do the same had you been here. But you can take my word for it that I have neither raped nor seduced Clarinda Bain.'

They went into the hotel, said good night to the porter, and got into the lift. They stood side by side. Cormac reached out and pressed the button for the fourth floor. They began to rise.

'So you're trying to tell me that nothing at all happened?' Alec had exchanged his headmasterly tone for a sly, suggestive one. He pulled the belt of his dressing gown in tight. 'That seems difficult to believe, Cormac. The girl's gone on you.'

The lift lurched to a stop and after giving a bit of a judder the door slid back to reveal the corridor plunged in darkness. Cormac groped for the wall switch and a weak light came on.

'Sorry to disappoint you, Alec,' he said. 'I'm afraid you'll have to find your own kicks.'

*Now on that last night in Paris, Mr Aherne, we believe that you were absent from the hotel for over an hour, with the girl in question. Would you like to tell us how you spent that hour?*

Cormac goes into the kitchen to rinse his own mug.

'Why wouldn't I approve?' he asks his daughter. 'Try me. What do you think I'd have against your boyfriend?'

'Everything.'

'Come now, I'm not that narrow-minded!'

Is she sleeping with him, whoever he is, this pimpled youth, or man of forty? The thought of the latter makes him gulp, but if this lover of hers were simply a boy from school she wouldn't be so desperate to conceal his identity, would she? He does too much talking to himself in his head.

If she is sleeping with him, whoever he might be, is she protecting herself? Alarm strikes at his heart. If anything bad should befall this beautiful daughter whom he loved from the moment he set eyes on her! He has a vision of her contracting some deadly disease, wasting away. His problem is that he has too much imagination, so the aunts used to say, all but Sal, who had been accused of the same crime herself when she was a child. The trouble is that his imagination is tending to become morbid now that he doesn't have anything but the making of sandwiches to occupy his mind. Obsessional thoughts about Sophie's boyfriend and Rachel's lover have occupied the empty space that used to be filled by his sculpture.

'You know not to take risks, don't you, Sophie?'

'I'm not stupid.'

'Are you -?' He breaks off. He cannot decide if he is justified in pressing her like this. But she is under age and he is her guardian, ill-equipped as he feels to guard her against anything. He presumes she must be sleeping with the boyfriend since she has not denied it.

'I'm almost sixteen,' she says. 'I could get married in Gretna Green soon. Or Edinburgh.' She smiles. 'I could leave school.'

He bites his tongue to stop himself delivering a lecture on the drawbacks of leaving school without qualifications, and how one would inevitably come to regret it in the future.

# Chapter Ten

Clarinda's sixteenth birthday fell the week after their
return from Paris.

She was waiting for him a few blocks from school,
in the doorway of an empty shop. He was on foot. She
knew his route home and he had not thought to vary
it. As soon as he saw her he realised that he should
have done. He should have anticipated this. Since coming back to school he had made sure that he was not
alone with her and in class tried to treat her like any
other pupil. He was aware, however, of the other
pupils' raised interest when he addressed her, which
he continued to do, since not to have done so would
have also had been noted.

The first class after their return had been especially
difficult for the pupils had understandably wanted to
talk about Paris. When it was Clarinda's turn and she
spoke of Gwen John there was some sniggering.
Cormac quickly moved the conversation onto more
general grounds, asking the pupils if they thought it
brought extra insight into an artist's work to know
something about their lives and see the environments
they had lived and worked in? Did they, for example,
think that their visit to Monet's garden had added
something to their viewing of the water lilies? Clarinda

was silent but he already knew what she thought; the rest seemed to think that the visit to Giverny had enhanced their appreciation of the paintings though they were all agreed that that was a bonus and not essential.

'I felt I was standing inside his picture,' said Cathy, surprising him. 'That one of the pond and the little green wooden bridge over it. It added something to it, at least that's what I thought,' she added diffidently.

One of the boys said he could understand that but he couldn't see what standing in front of 87 rue du Cherche-Midi gazing up at the facade of the fourth floor would do for anyone, especially when you didn't even know for sure which window it was! His remark was followed by some hilarity and the pink in Clarinda's cheeks darkened.

Listening to their summing up Cormac, as their teacher, had felt pleased with his students. Their interest and enthusiasm had increased as the week in Paris had advanced. In spite of everything - in spite of the bit of bother with Clarinda, which was how he was choosing to regard it - the trip had been worthwhile and he would be able to say so in all truth when he came to write his report. Some members of staff had been giving him odd looks - Alec McCaffy's tongue had doubtless been busy - but he felt hopeful that by the following week it would have become old news and something else would have happened to provide fodder for playground and staff room gossip.

Appearing from the shop doorway, Clarinda fell into step beside him. 'It's my birthday,' she said.

'*Clarinda!*'

'You could wish me many happy returns.'

'Happy birthday to you. Now, listen -'

'I'm sixteen, Cormac. I've come of age.'

'I'm pleased for you.'

'Don't be sarcastic. I don't like it when you are.'

He lengthened his stride and she broke into a trot to keep up with him.

'I need to talk to you, Cormac, *please!* I'm so unhappy I don't know what to do with myself.'

He did not feel particularly happy himself now and wished he could take a sabbatical, go to the other end of the earth, to Australia, or Bora-Bora, and return after a year to find Clarinda laughing about her crush on him.

'I want to talk to you, Cormac.' She was becoming tearful. How could they proceed along the road like this with the chance of being seen by dozens of pupils, as well as teachers? 'If you don't let me talk to you I'll do something awful.' She gulped. 'I'll throw myself off the Dean Bridge!'

He slowed his step. 'Now that's blackmail, Clarinda, and you know it. You have no intention of throwing yourself off anywhere.' She wouldn't, would she? You could never be sure with young girls. It reminded him of Sophie threatening to leave home. All right, they'd told her, go and pack your bag, and she hadn't of course, and they had known she wouldn't. But could he know for certain that Clarinda would not throw herself off the Dean Bridge in a moment of derangement? He remembered her going on about Gwen John tempting providence by sitting on rocks close to the sea and being swept off by a huge wave and referring to the sensation afterwards as 'delicious danger'. Clarinda had said she understood that. But surely danger was only delicious if you had at least a chance of survival? Throwing oneself off the Dean Bridge would not come into that category. He was not totally reassured, however.

Her bottom lip was quivering. 'You don't know how miserable I am.'

'What else can I say? I can only go on repeating myself, saying I'm sorry, and try to persuade you to put all this behind you.'

'I just want to be with you.' Her voice was dwindling to a peep. Suddenly she burst into a torrent of weeping.

'OK,' he said, 'let's go and have a cup of coffee and talk.'

She sniffled her tears away and dried her eyes on a tissue. He took her to a different cafe from the one they had gone to before.

*So, even after your return from Paris, Mr Aherne, you went to a cafe with her in Edinburgh? Was that not an odd thing to do considering the complications of the situation? Was it wise? You said you wished to discourage her.*

He ordered coffee for them both and a *pain au chocolat* for Clarinda, at her request. She was starving, she hadn't eaten all day. And no doubt *pain au chocolat* reminded her of Paris, not that she needed any reminding.

'I wish we could have stayed there. Why don't we just go back? We could! Why not?'

'Now don't talk daft!'

He noticed that she had blue marks underneath her eyes and wondered if her mother would have noticed them too.

'I was happy there. You said you were always happy when you returned to Paris. You said it made you feel fully alive and that is how I felt. You said it made the creative juices flow.'

'I've said a lot of things,' he said. 'Some of them dubious.'

Nothing you said about Paris was dubious.' She gazed limply at him. 'Cormac, don't be angry with me just because I fell in love with you.'

Cormac is watching his daughter fill a hot water bottle. She fills it carefully with water from the steaming kettle, then she holds it against her chest to squeeze out the air, and finally she screws in the top, getting the threads to match, taking her time, showing no sign of the impatience that she sometimes does. She takes a towel and dries the top. He is watching every movement, as if he might learn something about her. He has been so close to her all these years, yet now he feels he has to learn her anew, to try to understand the changes that she is going through.

'Night, Dad.' She kisses his cheek.

'Night, love.' He wants to hold her tight, to lock her away, so that she cannot come to any harm, but that is not an option.

'Clarinda -' He paused and took a deep breath. 'This cannot go on. You'll have to talk yourself out of it just as you talked yourself in. I can't take any more of it. I'm coming to the end of my tether.'

'But that *kiss*!'

'Was a mistake. It should not have happened!' It had been reprehensible of him to succumb, even for those few seconds. Repent! He could hear the aunts crying in his head.

'You're being unkind.' Clarinda's voice was on the waver again. 'And I told my mother that you were the nicest man I have ever met.'

'You will just have to tell her you were mistaken. Right now I feel I could become downright nasty. And I don't want to hear about Rodin being nasty to Gwen John, I've heard enough of it.'

'But, Cormac, don't you see ... it didn't *stop* her loving him. And he wasn't nasty to her all the time. Even though he had that other woman, that awful American duchess, he still came to visit her and make love to her. She said that if she had to go through a whole week without him making love to her she froze up like a stream in winter. I understand how that feels, I do. You shouldn't undervalue my love for you.'

He had his first premonition that she had talked to her mother.

'And don't please tell me how much older than me you are. Age has nothing to do with love.'

'It can often have quite a lot to do with it. You've lacked a father figure in your life. Don't you think you've seen me as some kind of substitute?'

'I don't feel like a daughter to you. I want to go to bed with you.'

He felt the heat gathering in his face. He glanced sideways at the people at the next table; they seemed very quiet, and not to be talking, which made him wonder if they were listening. Was the whole world listening? He felt there were eyes everywhere.

'It's true, Cormac. I do want to.'

He got up abruptly and went to the counter and

asked for the bill. The reckoning. Even then he did not think it would turn out to be so high. When he turned round he saw that Clarinda was crying into a paper tissue and the people at the next table were giving him dirty looks. If they had not overheard the conversation they might, with a bit of luck, think he was her father giving her a telling-off for coming home late.

He made for the door and she jumped up and ran after him. Out in the street he said, 'I'm saying it for the last time, Clarinda. I'm sorry about everything. But now we must draw a line under it. I think you're a lovely girl but I look on you as a daughter more than anything else.' She was continuing to cry but he did not even feel sorry for her any longer. He felt washed out. Arid. Incapable of feeling anything. His heart sat like a stone in his chest.

Later that evening, up in his studio, he paused from his work to go to the window and look down on the street and saw the silhouette of a girl standing under a tree opposite. He swore softly, over and over again. He did not know what else to do. It was dark and light rain was visible falling under the arc of a street light. She was looking up at his window. She had seen him. He pulled the blind down sharply, catching his finger, drawing blood. He sucked his finger and swore again.

He couldn't work now. He covered the piece he was working on, the figure of a young boy kneeling, his son kneeling, and went downstairs to pour himself a dram.

'What's up?' asked Rachel. 'Your hand's shaking. And have you cut your finger?'

'It's nothing. Only a scratch.' He remembered the angry marks left on Clarinda's bare arms outside the Métro at Clignancourt.

'You're shivering,' insisted Rachel.

He shook his head. That would have been the moment to tell her, but he didn't. It will all die down, he told himself; Clarinda will become bored and go away and forget about me and Paris and Gwen John and Rodin and return to her own life, to real life. Did he accept that what she said she felt was real? He did not know. He was too confused to judge the dividing line between fantasy and reality. He didn't want to think any more. He tossed back the whisky, pleasured by the sting in his throat, and poured himself another now that Rachel had gone upstairs to have a shower.

He went into the hall, quietly opened the front door and peered out into the damp night. His left-hand neighbour opened his door at the same time and called over the hedge, 'Is that you, Cormac? There's a girl been standing under that tree across the road all evening. I don't know what she thinks she's up to. I was thinking of calling the police. You can never tell with all these burglaries around.'

'Don't do that,' said Cormac hastily. 'I was just going out to have a word with her. She's a pupil at my school. She's a bit, well, disturbed.'

'Drugs?'

'Not sure.'

'Half the teenagers seem to be off the wall these days, one way or another. I don't envy you your job.'

The neighbour waited on his step while Cormac went down the path, unlatched the dripping gate with fumbling fingers, and crossed the road.

'I knew you'd come out to me,' said Clarinda, her cold blue face cracking into a smile. 'I knew you would-n't leave me here.'

200

'You have to go home, Clarinda.' He kept his voice down, conscious of his neighbour's straining ears. 'You can't stay out here and you can't come into my house.'

'I suppose your wife is there.'

'Yes, my wife is there.'

'We could go somewhere else.'

'We are going nowhere else.'

'I'm *sixteen* now.'

'I know. You've already told me.'

'But don't you see, I'm of *age*?'

'Need a hand, Cormac?' called the neighbour, coming down his garden path to the gate.

'No, no, it's fine, thanks, John. I'm just going to see her home. Right now, Clarinda, ' he said firmly when John had retreated, 'we are going!'

He took hold of her arm and pulled her away from the tree. After the first few reluctant steps she allowed him to lead her down the street.

'We could go up Calton Hill.'

'I am taking you home. Where do you live? And don't bother to give me the wrong address and lead me another merry dance for I'm not standing for it!'

'You're very angry.'

'Yes. Very.'

He walked with head down into the wind. Soon the rain came on. Drops of water clogged his eyelashes blurring the night. The traffic lights wavered and their reflections ran like spilled red, amber and green paint on the road. He could not go through another night like this; something had to be done to jolt her out of her madness. Next time she might bring a sleeping bag and camp out in his garden. He wondered if she had a cat. Mrs Bain looked the type of woman to have half a dozen.

It took twenty minutes hard walking to reach the street of the Bains. They lived in a typical, grey stone tenement block. Clarinda said they were hoping to move sometime - her mother would love a garden - but they would have to wait until they could afford something better.

'The neighbours think we're kind of eccentric. Just because we're different.' She was in a chatty mood now and appeared to be enjoying this late-night walk.

'Which number?' he asked.

'Are you coming to the door with me?'

'I'm going to wait till I see you go inside.'

'That's it there,' said Clarinda, indicating a dark greenish-coloured door in need of painting. 'We're on the top.'

Letting his eyes travel up Cormac saw that it was easy to pick out the Bains' dwelling. The windows glowed with a pinkish-orange light; one might almost have thought that the flat was on fire. Presumably Mrs Bain was still up and about and awaiting the return of her daughter.

'Right then,' he said, 'on you go. And don't do this again or you'll make me hate you.'

'Don't say that!'

'I'm tired, Clarinda. Very tired.'

'See you tomorrow,' she said.

He waited while she crossed the road and opened the door. Before vanishing inside she paused to look back at him. She waved but he did not respond.

As he was about to turn and go he glanced up again and saw a face appear at one of the flaming windows. He wondered if Mrs Bain knew where her daughter had gone and what she had been doing.

What exactly did she know? Was she encouraging Clarinda?

He went home.

Davy is in bed asleep and Cormac is restless. He makes a cup of coffee; he drinks a half glass of wine left at the bottom of a bottle and makes a wry face at its sourness; he goes out to stand on the top step with his arms folded across his chest, allowing the night wind to ruffle his hair. He can't stop thinking about Sophie and wondering what she is up to. The bruise that she has underneath her eye - is her boyfriend violent? Then there's that mouldy smell that she often gives off when she comes in. He decides to phone Rachel and have a chat with her about it; at least that will be his excuse for he does have another agenda running at the same time. And he misses having her to talk to; she was always able to get things into perspective more easily than he and had a way of defusing a situation. He dials her number and waits. The ringing sound goes on and on; he lets it ring longer than he normally would. He imagines the machine sitting on the hall table beside a vase of flowers - she likes to have fresh cut flowers in the house as well as pot plants, all of which in her care flourish and bloom like the lilies in the field, whereas he tends to forget about his and they end up looking sad and dejected - and he imagines the living room empty of people but warm and inviting with cushions plumped and surfaces dust-free. She is obviously out, as must be Sophie, and they have forgotten to put on the answering machine. He is about to put down the receiver when Rachel answers. He has not been expecting it after the delay and is taken by surprise. She sounds a little breathless, as if she has just run up the outside stair and flung open the door to grab the receiver.

'Yes?' Normally she would say, 'Rachel Aherne here' in a composed voice.

'Hi,' he says. 'It's me.'

'Oh hello, Cormac.' She sounds guarded. Or is he imagining it?

'Were you out?'

'No, no. Just upstairs.' So she was *upstairs?* That makes him pause.

Does it take that long to come down such a short flight of stairs? Unless she was having a shower. But she did not say that she was, which would have been the natural thing to say. Is she with someone? Is there a man standing behind her, touching her? Now his imagination has something else to work on. Rachel is waiting for him to tell her the reason for his call.

'I was just wondering about Sophie. If you'd managed to find out anything more about what she's up to?'

'No, I haven't.' She sounds un interested. Is the man caressing her, urging her to turn back into his arms?

'Is she in?'

'No, she went to Tilda's. She should be back soon.'

'Oh, Tilda's.' He can think of nothing else to detain her. 'See you Sunday then, as usual.'

'As usual,' she says, and the call is over.

He is even more restless now. He goes upstairs and pushes open the door of Davy's room. The boy is lying on his back sound asleep with one arm curled round his head. When he sleeps he has seldom been known to wake. Cormac tiptoes back downstairs and puts on a jacket, then he quietly lets himself out of the flat.

He covers the short stretch of road that separates the two streets in seconds. On the corner of Rachel's street he comes to a halt. Cautiously he peers round the corner. Nothing seems to be happening. Cars are parked, curtains are drawn, not even a dog is barking. The street is too narrow to loiter in, unless one is prepared to crouch behind a car. As he watches he sees a movement half way down. Someone is coming down an outside staircase. He thinks it might be Rachel's. He retreats back round the corner and keeps in close to the wall. There are no houses on the opposite side the road, only the Glenogle swimming baths, and the steep steps called Gabriel's Road that lead up to the lane behind Saxe Coburg Place. There is no one to observe him acting suspiciously, unless the winged angel Gabriel himself is hovering above. He listens, hears an engine revving up, and after a few seconds a car nudges its rear end out into the main road with its back light indicating that it intends to turn right. Cormac pulls in his stomach and flattens himself as close to the wall as possible. The car looks familiar. Very familiar. Can it be? It is continuing to back out, is reversing now round the corner, towards him; and he can see the dark bulky outline of the driver, half turned in his seat to look out of the back window. For a moment the car and its driver rest there and he wonders if he has been seen, and identified; then they start to move, to gather speed, and they are off, sweeping away in the opposite direction. Cormac steps into the middle of the pavement and watches until the car's rear lights have dwindled into the gloom. He could swear that the car belongs to Archie Gibson, his former headmaster.

'What came over you last night?' Rachel asked, the morning after he had frog-marched Clarinda back to her street.

'How do you mean?'

'Going out for a walk at that hour? Without even your coat on.'

That might have been another chance to tell her about Clarinda had the children not been there, but they were, sitting hunched over the table yawning and complaining that they weren't hungry and didn't see why they should be *made* to eat when they weren't. There was no chance of taking Rachel aside, either, for they would all have to get going in ten minutes, and his story was not one that could be told in a hurry. He said he'd felt restless.

'That's not new, is it? But you didn't even have your coat on.'

'I went on the spur of the moment.'

Rachel did not look convinced. She turned her attention to Davy, who was fiddling with his cereal but not eating. They heard the letter box flap snap shut announcing the arrival of the post, which gave Sophie the chance to leave the table to go and fetch it.

'Three for you, Mum. One for Dad. Peachy paper. Wow! Who's writing to you on that? Not Granny, though. And it smells of' - she sniffed - 'patchouli.'

'It's probably some pupil or other,' said Cormac hurriedly, taking the envelope and shoving it half under his plate.

'Aren't you going to open it?'

'I haven't time.' He rose, abandoning the last of his coffee and putting the envelope in his pocket. Rachel was looking curious.

He went up to the bathroom and locked the door. It reminded him of the first time a girl had sent him a Valentine. He'd been fourteen and he'd gone into the bathroom to read it without his mother's eyes watching him. When he'd come out she'd said, 'I've no time for the kind of girl that runs after a boy. She must have no pride.' Cormac had said nothing. He'd sent the girl a Valentine himself.

'Darling Cormac,' Clarinda had written, 'since I can't see you every minute of every day and every night the only way I can talk to you is by writing to you. I can't forget those wonderful times we had together in Paris, especially the night that you kissed me. I shall never forget <u>The Kiss</u>.' 'The Kiss' was firmly underlined.

He took the peachy-pink letter and its matching envelope and shredded them into tiny pieces and dropped them like confetti into the toilet. Then he flushed them away. He had no chance to speak to Clarinda on her own in school that day and he had taken his bicycle to work so that he was able to make a quick getaway afterwards.

The following morning, there was another letter. This one had been delivered by hand, before the post came. He saw the pink rectangle lying on the brown doormat when he came downstairs. He had come down early, deliberately. With a quick glance up the stairs he bent down and picked up the envelope. He was somewhat surprised that Clarinda would opt for pink notepaper. A liking inherited from her mother, perhaps? Opening the door he peered cautiously round it, afraid that she might be standing on the step. But she was not. She must have slipped up the path, and slipped away again. Did her mother know that she'd left home so early in the morning? What did she know? It was time he went and talked to the woman. Clarinda was not standing under the tree across the road, either. He went as far as the gate and glanced up and down the street. There appeared to be no sign of her at all.

'Not a bad morning,' called over John, his next-door neighbour, who was coming down his path, freshly shaved and spruced up, the toes of his shoes glinting as he stepped smartly out. He always went to work early, walking all the way up town. He had told Cormac he liked to get into the office before anyone else to have time to settle himself in peace. Cormac found the idea attractive but somehow or other never seemed to manage it himself. Mornings in their household tended to be hassled.

'Not bad,' agreed Cormac automatically, suddenly becoming aware that he was out in his pyjamas and slippers and that he was clutching a pink envelope in his hand and his neighbour was eyeing it and him curiously. 'Have a good day,' he muttered and went back inside. He was tempted to chuck the blasted envelope and its contents down the toilet without opening it but found he could not resist reading what she had written. She had penned a long description about her room so that, she said, he would be able to envisage it.

'I am going to do a painting of my room. I've started to make some sketches which I'd love to show you. I plan to make the composition simple: just a small table with a vase of brilliant dahlias (my mother is always buying flowers) and a chair by the window. I know it might seem that I am just copying Gwen John but my interpretation will be different. You would say so yourself, wouldn't you? But I do think Gwen was right not to overcrowd her paintings.' He groaned and started shredding.

Someone was rattling the door handle. 'Dad, are you going to be in there all day!' demanded Sophie.

When Cormac did come to tell Rachel about Clarinda, after he'd been suspended, she said he should have kept the letters, as evidence that the girl was pursuing him.

*You say the girl wrote letters to you, Mr Aherne. Why did you not keep them? Did you think they might incriminate you?*

He is convinced that the car he has just seen coming out of Rachel's street was Archie Gibson's, and that the man driving was the headmaster himself. He must have been to call on Rachel. What other reason would he have for being in that particular street? Perhaps it had merely been a friendly call. *Just passing, thought I'd drop in, see how you were doing, for old times sake.* No, he cannot convince himself of that.

*This isn't going to be easy for me, Cormac.* Thus spake his former friend and head teacher on that fateful day when he was suspended. The words ring in Cormac's ears as he retraces his steps back to his own street; they have attained a new significance. 'This isn't easy for me now, Archie,' he mutters. He remembers the day after their return from Paris, sitting in the pub with Archie, telling him about Clarinda, how enthusiastic she was about art, and Gwen John, trying to build up to finally telling him - Telling him what? Everything? Would he have told him about the kiss?

'Funny business, isn't it,' he had begun, 'what attracts one person to another? It's not totally physical, is it?'

Archie looked startled, and guilty. Yes, guilty. But Cormac only realises that after he has seen the headmaster's car leaving Rachel's street. What had Archie said in response? He can't remember. Perhaps nothing. And he himself, wrapped up in his own thoughts, might not have noticed.

'*Dad*!' He hears Davy's voice as he unlocks the door. 'Where have you *been*? I was calling for you. I thought you'd gone.'

Cormac gathers his son into his arms. 'It's all right, Davy, I'm here. You know I'd never go away. I just went down into the street for a breath of air. I didn't think you'd wake.'

'I had a horrible dream. I was coming home from school and I couldn't find the house ...'

'There, now, it was only a dream. You know you won't ever have to look for the house when you're coming home from school. I'll always be there to meet you.' Every day at three o'clock he is committed to standing at the school gate. He resolves to be sharper in future. Sometimes Davy is there before him, frowning, peering anxiously up the street.

He gives Davy a drink of hot milk and puts him back to bed; he waits beside him until he falls asleep again.

*Rachel and Archie Gibson.*

He goes to the phone and presses redial. Rachel answers in her more gathered-together voice.

'Oh, hello, Cormac. Sophie's home, you'll be glad to know. She came in five minutes ago. Do you want to speak to her?'

'No, I was wondering if you could give me Archie's number.'

'Archie?' Her voice has shifted a register, and sounds splintered. He is listening with intent, ready to catch every nuance.

'Yes, Archie Gibson's. I no longer have it on me, I think it was probably in the family book you took with you.'

'He's moved, actually. He and Sheila split up, you know. She stayed in the house.'

'Perhaps you could give me their old number and I'll get Archie's new one from her.'

'Were you wanting it for any reason in particular?' She is trying to sound casual.

Cormac says he just thought it would be nice to meet up for a drink. Old times' sake and all that. He and Archie go back quite a way, after all. They shared a flat when they were students. *What else have they shared?*

'Oh yes, of course,' says Rachel, 'hang on a minute.' She is confused at the other end of the line, is rustling through pages and can't seem to put her finger on it. 'It's in an awful mess, this book, with things written in and others scored out, I've been meaning to get a new one and throw this out but it's such a bother transferring all the numbers.'

He waits until she has no option but to give him the number he wants. 'Sheila's out a lot,' she warns him. He can always leave a message, he says.

Sheila happens to be in and gives him Archie's number though he has to listen to a long story before she does. She does not mention Rachel. 'He was having it off with someone while we were still together, oh yes! He thought I didn't know - men are such fools, sorry about that, Cormac - but how could I not know? A woman always knows. He started shaving twice a day and he bought himself a whole load of new boxer shorts. He usually hung on to his underwear until it reached the disgusting stage and I would have to throw it out myself when it came through in the wash.' Cormac does not want to know any more of these details but Sheila is a difficult woman to stop. He half-listens, then when she pauses he asks, 'Did you ever find out who he was having the affair with?'

'Oh, no, he was far too clever for that. He is clever, is Archie. And he had to keep up his image as the virtuous, unsullied headmaster, didn't he?'

When Cormac has extricated himself he makes his final call of the evening. While he's dialling and waiting he reflects what a big thing the telephone has become in his life, one of his chief lines of communication, whereas, before, he seldom answered it, if he could avoid it.

'Archie Gibson speaking.'

'Hi, Archie. It's me, Cormac.'

'Oh, hello, Cormac.' Archie is not surprised, nor does he ask how he got hold of his number. So Rachel has phoned to warn him; she had time to do that while he was talking to Sheila. 'Nice to hear from you,' says Archie. 'How're you doing?'

'Fantastic! Sandwiches are big these days. I'll soon be floating the business on the stock market. I'll cut you in on the early shares if you like.'

Archie gives a relieved laugh.

Cormac suggests meeting for that drink they talked about.

'Can you get out in the evenings? I mean, I thought you had Davy living with you?'

'I do but I can't sit in every evening. Rachel babysits

when I want to go out. I'm sure she'd do it for us. I told her I was going to give you a call.'

'Oh, you did?'

'So how about it?'

Archie says he'd like to go for a drink but not right now, he's afraid, he's up to his eyes, working at home every evening, trying to catch up, Cormac knows what a load of paperwork he has these days, all this bloody bureaucracy, and he's in the middle of some special reports that have to be in by next week.

'I get the picture,' says Cormac.

Archie promises to give him a ring once he's managed to clear his feet a bit. 'I don't suppose I'll ever get them totally clear,' he remarks.

'It'd be a lot to ask for,' says Cormac, and puts the phone down.

*Rachel and Archie Gibson.*

# Chapter Eleven

'Bain,' he read on the bell at the top of the row. He paused to take a deep breath before putting his finger to it. He would need all the wind he could muster. A prayer wouldn't go amiss either but he couldn't think of a suitable one. The time had come to try to take control of the situation, instead of waiting passively for the storm to pass overhead. Clarinda, he knew, would be at school, rehearsing for *Midsummer Night's Dream*, the school play, in which she was to play Titania. The drama teacher said she was going to be brilliant in the role, just as she had been as Ophelia last year. She had great range. A very talented girl. He thought she could go on the stage.

After what seemed a long moment the voice of Mrs Bain floated out through the grill at the side of the door.

'Yes? Who is it, please?'

'It's Cormac Aherne,' he said gruffly.

'Sorry, I didn't quite catch that.' Was she trying to torment him? Her voice was clear enough to him and he thought it had sounded amused.

'Cormac Aherne,' he bellowed. 'Clarinda's art teacher.'

'Ah, Mr Aherne! You may come up.'

'Thank you,' he muttered and on hearing the door buzz gave it a hard shove and he was in.

He stubbed his shins on a bicycle as he went up the ill-lit passage; he then had to skirt round a couple of pushchairs badly parked at the foot of the stairs. A pungent smell of cat made his nose wrinkle. He did not blame the Bains for wanting to move to a garden. He began his climb of the steep grey stairs. When he reached the second landing he had to pause for a second to draw a longer breath, although he had hoped not to. It would seem to put him at a disadvantage if he were to arrive short of wind and stiff-limbed.

He started on the next flight before he was fully recovered. Halfway there, he could not resist glancing up. She was waiting for him outside her door, clad in a purple and orange kimono that made a brilliant show of colour against her drab surroundings. She was looking down on him and he, unfortunately, was stuck with looking up at her. He was definitely at a disadvantage now. Making a supreme effort he went briskly up the last few steps.

'Quite a climb, isn't it?' she said gaily.

'Quite.'

'But, Mr Aherne, this is a real surprise!' He had the feeling that it was not an overwhelming one. She reminded him of a spider who has been awaiting her prey, confident that it would be drawn in, all in good time. The hand holding the door was barnacled with large heavy rings. Knuckledusters. She might well want to sock him in the jaw once he'd said his piece.

'Mrs Bain,' he said, 'I have to talk to you. Clarinda has some ridiculous notions in her head.'

'Ridiculous, Mr Aherne? That is not what I've been hearing.'

In spite of what would seem to be incriminating evidence, Cormac wonders if his suspicion about Rachel and Archie Gibson is ridiculous. Surely Archie, who was his friend for twenty years and more and whom he saw in school, day in, day out, would not have betrayed him in this way? How could he have managed to look him in the eye over their after-school half-pints and talk normally about normal things? Cormac tries to think back to that time, to conjure up the pub, the corner where they used to sit round the side of the bar. He can remember nothing of significance, no clue unintentionally dropped on Archie's part that should have alerted him. They mostly talked shop, as far as he can remember.

He is raking his memory, too, about Rachel. Perhaps she never did go to the French conversation class, or to meet her friend Marcia. Perhaps every time she left the house in the evening she went to meet his headmaster. Whenever she was going out, even if it were to a class, she would always change out of her work clothes. She likes to be well dressed. He can see her with her dark hair brushed and gleaming, poised to leave. 'Won't be late,' she'd call up. He'd come to the top of the stairs to see her. 'Have a good time,' he'd call complacently down and return to the piece of work that was absorbing him. There was no doubt he had allowed himself to become too absorbed.

Where did they conduct their secret meetings, Rachel and Archie Gibson? It couldn't have been easy, with both of them having public as well as private faces, liable to be recognised by any number of people. He remembers now that she had played a lot of tennis that spring and summer; two or three nights a week, in fact. He remarked on it at the time, said, 'You must be keeping fit!' She belonged to the same club as Archie! He read nothing into that at the time. When she'd come in he'd ask if she'd seen Archie and she'd say casually but quite often, 'Actually we played a game of mixed doubles together.' She and Archie would be well matched at tennis; both had fast serves and strong backhand returns. Did it all start in full view of the world, on the open courts, brushing hands as they passed tennis balls one to the other, exchanging covert glances? And then what? Where did they go? They couldn't have got up to much in the clubhouse. How long *did* the affair actually go on? She said they'd only been together two or three times; she meant sexually, he presumed. Was it serious, this relationship, or a fling to break the boredom of their marriages? Had she been bored with her marriage?

Questions rattle in his skull like hard peas in a drum. He put those questions to Rachel on the night she made her confession but she would not reveal anything but the bare fact. She had had an affair, which was now over, and she was sorry. But was she sorry that she had hurt him or sorry that she had had an affair? He did not ask any further questions for she would not be drawn; she would not cave in eventually as he would have done in a similar situation and said, 'All right, I'll tell you, since you want to know.' She could contain herself better.

'Sometimes things come out of the blue and take you by surprise,' she said. She frowned, as as if she were trying to understand why they did. She would not have liked being taken by surprise.

'True,' he agreed. 'There was my father who had an affair with Mrs Blaney at her B&B, and then he upped and left us. That took us by surprise.'

'It was good, though,' said Rachel. 'that you saw your dad again before he died.'

She had been ironing and listening to a Radio 4 programme one evening when she'd heard an announcement that had made her drop the iron.

Would Cormac Patrick Aherne, formerly of Belfast, and believed to be living somewhere in the United Kingdom, please get in touch with Manchester Royal. Infirmary, where his father, Patrick Seamus Aherne, is dangerously ill.'

He drove through the early hours of the morning down the M6, praying that his father would still be alive when he got there, and he was. A priest was just leaving, having administered the last rites.

Pat Aherne recognised his son, not the forty-four year-old man seated at his bedside, but the voice of the boy he'd known as a child. 'I can hear you there all right, son. I'd have known you anywhere. I've often wondered what you were like. I wrote to you, you know, several times, oh yes, 'deed I did, but the letters came back marked 'Not known here' in your mother's hand. Ah well, who could blame her, poor woman? She didn't get much of a deal from me but there's nothing I can do about it now. Tell me about yourself, son. I want to know it all. Have you children of your own?'

Cormac held his father's hand and recounted the story of his life from aged ten to forty-four. As the minutes ticked quietly past he built up a picture of a man contented with his lot, living in a desirable house in a desirable neighbourhood, holding down a decent job, which he was at that time, an important job involving the education of the young, also gradually building a reputation as a sculptor for himself, married to a lovely woman with a good job, with two wonderful children to show for it, a girl and a boy, both blessed with brains and looks. Of course he was selective. When relating a story one had to be, and so he introduced no element into his tale that was not ideal. Pat Aherne could sleep peacefully now, reassured that by abandoning his child he had not blighted his life. His son was a success story. After a while he sank into a coma though the nurse said to carry on talking for one never knew how much they took in when they were in an unconscious state. Cormac stayed at the bedside for the rest of the day, with Mrs Blaney. They each held a hand of the dying man and were with him at the end.

'Go with God, Pat Aherne,' said Mrs Blaney, making the sign of the cross over the soft pillow of her breast. 'You've made me a happy woman and may you rest in peace.'

Cormac wondered if anyone would do the same for him when he went. Rachel was no stronger a believer than himself though she was firmer about her disbelief than he and seemed not to have the same feeling of a void within her. She said life itself was enough for her whereas a bit of him kept hoping that there might be something else. He'd always wanted to have his cake and eat it! So his mother would have said.

'He was a lovely man, your da,' said Mrs Blaney.

Cormac enfolded her in his arms and they shed their tears together.

'It was great you made it before he went,' said Mrs Blaney later when they sat in a pub having a Bushmills together.

Cormac had time now to feel angry with his mother. Mrs Blaney said she'd not been too pleased with her herself.

'When Pat was brought into the hospital I got her number from Directory Enquiries and phoned her. I asked her to pass the message on to you. She said she'd never heard of a Patrick Aherne. That was why I asked them to put it on the wireless.'

After he went home Cormac had a furious row on the phone with his mother who wept and asked forgiveness. 'But think what he did to us, son.'


'Are you trying to tell me that you have given my daughter no encouragement, Mr Aherne?' said Mrs Bain, who stood with one hand parked on her orange and purple satin hip.

They were both standing. She had invited him in. She had said, 'I think you should come in off that draughty landing and we will discuss this in a civilised manner. We don't want an argy-bargy, do we?' That had given him hope and encouraged him to think that she would not simply rail against him but would try to see his point of view. As soon as he had stepped over her threshold, however, and entered her boudoir - it was the word that came straight into his mind - he began to feel apprehensive. *Come into my parlour* ... The walls were hung with Eastern prayer mats; various tinkling baubles hung from the ceiling; the orange and pink lamps gave the room a warm if rather hectic glow; and there was a smell of joss sticks. The only furniture was a white piano and several large satin floor cushions spangled with tiny mirrors that flashed and winked and confused the eye. On top of the piano stood Robert Burns gazing steadily out of his frame into this cave of Eastern promise.

'Do you think, Mrs Bain,' said Cormac, struggling to stay calm, 'that I would actively encourage your daughter to look on me as anything other than her teacher? What do you take me for?'

'A man.' She seemed pleased with her response.

'Apart from anything else, I am forty-three.'

'A dangerous age for a man. Especially an attractive one.' She smiled now, making him wonder if he did not prefer her anger. 'You must be aware that you are attractive to women?' She was saying 'women' now, not 'girls'. Did she fancy him herself? Was she going to offer herself to him in place of her daughter? This was entering the realm of the bizarre. He had obviously made a mistake by coming here and trying to engage in any kind of rational dialogue with this fool of a woman. She was still looking at him with that cat-that-got-the cream-like smile. Their cat had looked like that yesterday after it had devoured a mouse and left its innards on the kitchen floor. But Clarinda's mother had not eaten him yet, his innards were intact. He rallied himself and took refuge in a little pomposity.

'I am married, Mrs Bain, and happily so, and I am nearly thirty years older than your daughter. She is only a year older than my own daughter.'

'That never stopped a man. My husband was twenty-two years older than me *and* he was married to someone else at the time. It didn't stop him seducing me.'

'I have not seduced your daughter.'

'That is not what she tells me.'

'She is suffering from an over-excited imagination, stimulated, I fear, by you, Mrs Bain.'

'What *do* you mean, Mr Aherne?'

'I think perhaps you tend towards the romantic and the dramatic -' He waved his hand vaguely at the room. He shouldn't have started on this tack; she could only take umbrage.

'You use that word 'romantic' as a slur, I rather think, to put me down. Oh yes, you do! I know your type. What is wrong with romance, tell me! Why should people not enjoy it? This ugly world could do with more of it. All this harping on the sordid does nothing for the soul. In Scotland we are bombarded with the under-belly of life as if nothing else was relevant. It can't be true unless we are rubbing our noses in the gutter! Drugs, gang rapes, degradation. How boring it all is. The Russians give proper recognition to the soul; their great writers acknowledge it, as well as the ordinary people. Why do we not? We don't want to look at our souls. We don't want to admit to having such things. We're afraid to feel too much. We're afraid to allow tenderness and romance into our lives. But the poetry of our great bard is romantic, is it not? What about the novels of Jane Austen? Are they not romances, in the best sense of the word? Can you say otherwise?' He was not being given the chance to say anything even though he had made a couple of attempts to put a word in, but there was no way in which he would be able to staunch her flow, short of smacking his hands together and shouting 'Enough!' in her face. Her indignation showed no sign of cooling. 'I am a keen supporter of the arts, Mr Aherne, let me tell you. I am a Friend of the Edinburgh Festival. I paint. I go to exhibitions. I take Clarinda to the opera and the ballet when I can afford it, which may not be often since prices are high, and I am a single parent. I love literature. I go to the Book Festival and listen to writers talking about themselves and their works. I go to the theatre. Is all of that a crime?'

'Yes, all right, Mrs Bain, I take your point, I might even agree with you to a certain degree, but let's get back to Clarinda.'

'I did not think you would answer any of my points and you have not.' She was wearing her smile again. He wanted to strangle her. 'But, yes, do let us get back to Clarinda. Her happiness is the most important thing in my life. More important than my own life.'

'And her wellbeing, as a student, is important to me, but purely as a student.'

'And you expect me to believe that? Come, come, Mr Aherne, let us be honest with each other. She told me you spent time alone in Paris together. Can you deny that?'

'It was by accident, not design.'

'Accident? But more than once? And late at night? Really, you must think I am very naive.'

'She ran off. I had to go after her. She was going crazy.'

'Why, I wonder? She is normally a very calm girl. Something must have upset her.'

'She'd allowed herself to become obsessed with the relationship between Gwen John and Rodin, that's why. You must know that. She's bound to have talked to you about it.'

'We are very close. We share our interests so naturally she did. We're more like sisters than mother and daughter.'

He had thought he would hear that at some point or other. He hoped she was not waiting for a compliment for none would be forthcoming. It might be politic for him to hand her one but he could not bend his pride to do it.

'I don't think we can lay *all* the blame on Gwen John,' she went on, 'do you? Why was it you who went after Clarinda and not the other teacher? Did you feel personally responsible for her?'

'As a matter of fact I did. I would be expected to. Since she is a pupil of mine -'

'Indeed.'

'They paused.

'My daughter tells me everything,' said Clarinda's mother.

'You are not foolish enough to believe that, are you, Mrs Bain? Or to believe everything she tells you?'

It was a mistake, of course, yet another, for him to have spoken to Mrs Bain in such a contemptuous fashion, not that he had actually intended his remark to convey contempt, but she certainly took it as such. She dropped her hand from her shiny hip to face him more squarely.

'You are not suggesting that my daughter is a liar, are you, Mr Aherne?'

'I'm not suggesting anything. It is for you to decide whether your daughter speaks the truth or not.'

'Exactly.' Now she folded her arms under her billowing bosom. That was how he saw her, billowing, floating in orange and purple satin, like an over-coloured, gaudy witch. He noticed that the motifs adorning her were dragons. They shimmered as her body moved with indignation beneath them. 'I think,' she said, 'that I am the person best equipped to decide whether my daughter can be trusted to tell the truth or not.'

Even then he did not think she would go to the police.

'If you'll excuse me, Mrs Bain, I must go home.'

'I won't excuse you anything, Mr Aherne,' said Clarinda's mother.

Next afternoon, he was summoned to the headmaster's office.

*Rachel and Archie Gibson.*

Come to think of it, they might have been better suited from the start. They had both gone to similar, independent, fee-paying schools and lived in similar leafy suburban roads with walled gardens, and Archie's father had been a lawyer while Rachel's plied his merchant banking trade. Their families would have been better pleased had they chosen each other than with the choices that they did make. Archie's mother was never able to abide his wife Sheila; she found her loud. So did Cormac, in fact, though he feels more sympathetic towards her now than he ever has. He wonders if Archie might not have fancied Rachel in the very beginning but he, Cormac, saw her first and asked her out and Archie was too honourable a man to cut in on a friend's woman. He remembers once saying jokingly to Rachel, 'I don't know why you didn't marry Archie. He'd have been a better bet. He's a steady chap, he earns a regular wage, and he comes from a good home.' 'I didn't want Archie,' she replied. 'It was you I wanted.'

226

Rachel rings after Davy is in bed and says she was thinking she might pop round for a chat, would that be all right? Fine, he replies, he's not doing anything in particular. He seldom is these evenings now that he no longer has essays to mark or his studio to retreat to. Did he use it too much as a retreat when they were together? Once when they were having a row she accused him of cutting himself off from the family when it suited him, especially if there was a problem in the offing. See you shortly, she says before ringing off. They agreed before they separated to remain friends so why should she not pop round when she feels like it? This is the first time that she has.

Hurriedly he removes the dirty cups from the sitting room and punches the cushions. He is dusting the mantelpiece when he hears her step on the outside stair. He shoves the duster behind a cushion.

She is carrying a bottle of Burgundy. It looks a good one, he remarks as he takes it from her. It's just what she happened to have in the house, she says. He takes it through to the kitchen to open it and fetch wine glasses. Archie is a keen wine buff, buys all his wine through a club. When they used to go to dinner with him and Sheila he would give them a little spiel about it, which vineyard it came from and all that. Cormac wonders if this bottle came from Archie's stock. He puts it on a tray with the glasses and carries it through.

Rachel is on her feet with her back to the room looking out of the window though there is nothing unusual to see, only a mirror-image house across the way.

'Here we are,' he says brightly.

She turns, gives him a half-smile and sits on the settee. She's nervous, which is not like her. She takes a

227

large swallow of wine and then says, 'I've come to talk to you.'

'I didn't expect you to say silent!'

'No, seriously talk, I mean.'

'Sophie?'

'No, me.'

'You're not ill?' He is alarmed.

She shakes her head. 'You're not going to like this,' she says and he knows he is not so he gulps down the rest of his wine and refills his glass from Archie's bottle.

'The affair that I had,' she begins and stops. 'Well, I would never tell you who the man was because it would have upset you too much. But I think you've guessed. I'm very sorry, Cormac.'

They drink in silence for a few minutes. A wind has sprung up outside and the window is rattling. He must do something about the frame. All the windows need attention, he ought to be getting on with it now that he has time. When he was still sculpting he wasn't much use in the house as a do-it-yourself man. Rachel used to do the decorating herself, said she'd rather than wait for him to get round to it.

'I guess I wasn't all that great as a husband.'

'That's not true. You mustn't think that. Anyway, it's not that simple. It never could be.'

'Artists are pretty self-centred though, aren't they?'

'Well, Rodin was, anyway. I don't suppose he ever did any washing up.'

That makes them laugh and they relax a little. He then asks, 'Was it really over when you said it was, your affair?'

She nods. 'And that was the way it stayed until we

228

separated. I hadn't intended it to start up all over again. He came round to see me ...' She shrugs. 'And, well, we realised that we were still strongly attracted to each other.'

She is free to do whatever she wants now, without excuse or apology, or need for concealment. As he is. But he does not know what he wants to do: that is the rub. He does not know how to begin again. He is less sure now than he was at seventeen; then, he was single-minded, on stream to do amazing things.

'Were you not attracted at all to Clarinda?' asks Rachel. 'You always said you weren't.'

And she never quite believed him. That had caused another little crack in their marriage. Their trust in each other had gradually begun to erode. In bed they had stayed more and more often on their own sides, with their backs turned, tucked away inside their own private thoughts, whereas, before, they had always liked to chat before sleeping.

'I don't know.' He is trying to think back to how he felt then. 'I could see that she was attractive but she was so *young*.'

'That was what you always said. You were flattered though?'

'I suppose I was.'

'You accepted her flattery? You didn't try to squash it?'

'Not soon enough.' Not until she had become obsessed, and by then it was too late. That was his first mistake.

'But you never laid a finger on her?'

He pauses, then says, 'I kissed her.' It is the first time he has admitted it to anyone other than himself.

*Mr Aherne, the girl in question maintains that you first kissed her outside the railway station at Montparnasse. Do you deny that?*

He did deny it, since the implication, he told himself, in an effort to justify his lie, was that he had gone on to kiss her on other occasions. He knew that it was going to be his word against hers. And he had more at stake than she had. To try to save himself he had to lie. But while telling the lie he could feel himself beginning to sweat. He had been brought up to regard the telling of a falsehood as a sin, and he still did. It was deeply embedded in him, this early teaching. He remembered that the French philosopher Henri Hude said that the first sin is to have no sense of sin. At least he did not have to plead guilty to that one! He wanted to take out his handkerchief and mop his forehead but feared that if he did his interrogators would take it as an admission of guilt.

They finish the bottle of wine, or rather Cormac finishes it. Rachel has only drunk a glass.

'Do you plan to live with him?' asks Cormac.

'Oh, no, it's too early for that. And it would be difficult for him while we were both still married.'

'A man in his position!'

'Well, yes. And there's Sophie to consider.'

They consider Sophie, a mystery to them both. They have no idea what is going on in her head. Now Davy, that is a different matter; he tells them what he is thinking, he protests, he complains, he says I don't want to do this, I want to do that. They are on safer ground with this conversation; their children are a unifying force.

Rachel gets up, yawning. 'I must go. You never know,

our daughter might have come home! And, by the way, Cormac, any time you want to go out in the evening I'll keep Davy. You should go out more often. I still do care about you, you know. I'd like you to be happy and not just to assuage my own guilt!' She gives him a rueful smile, then she leans over to kiss his cheek, and in the next instant has gone.

He drops Archie Gibson's empty wine bottle into the bin.

Next day, he sees their daughter. At least he is fairly certain that he has seen her though when he phones Rachel afterwards to tell her she questions it.

'Are you sure, Cormac?'

Davy was going to a friend's birthday party after school so Cormac took the opportunity to go up to the public library on George IV Bridge. He has started to read more now that he has the evenings after eight o'clock to himself. He drifted up the stairs to the art department without thinking and finding himself standing outside the door wondered what he was doing there. He was about to turn and go back down when he thought better of it. He pushed open the door and went in. He picked up a magazine and sat down at a table. And then he saw that he was sitting opposite Clarinda Bain.

'Don't go,' she said. 'I don't bite.' A smile flickered across her face.

'What are you reading?' he asked after a moment.

She displayed the cover. It was a book about the Pre-Raphaelites.

'Pretty romantic,' he commented. He felt sure Mrs Bain must have some postcards in her domain somewhere.

Perhaps in the bathroom where she could gaze at them from her peach-foamed bath.

'There's nothing wrong with the Romantic movement,' said Clarinda. He was struck by how much she had matured in the past year. She had left school after the fuss and gone to a Further Education college to do her Highers. She went on, 'It had its attractions. Still has. All great art does, doesn't it? You said that yourself in class.'

'You have too good a memory.'

She smiled again. 'I've applied to the Slade.'

'Good. Not easy to get in, but you might as well shoot for the top of the tree.'

'You told us that too.'

He shifted uncomfortably on his seat. Those, like Clarinda, who listened to and absorbed his words, must wonder what he was doing now, making sandwiches.

'Yes, OK, Gwen John went to the Slade. That's what you're thinking, isn't it? But that's not the reason, or the whole reason, anyway. I love her work but I shan't attempt to copy her style. It's too finicky for me, too miniaturist. I like something bigger and bolder.'

'I know you do. You enjoy vivid colour more than she did.'

It was easy to slip back into talking to her about things that interested them both; they had talked a lot, he realised, in the classroom after hours when the rest of the class had gone, as well as in the streets of Paris. This was no place to go on talking. People were reading quietly, making notes, glancing at them. He would have liked to have asked her to have a cup of coffee with him but he knew it would be a mistake. There

232

was no way forward with this; she was too young even though she might not think so herself, but she would, sometime.

He got up. 'I need to get back for my son. Good luck, Clarinda.'

He left her sitting with her book on the Pre-Raphaelites.

He took the Playfair Steps going down the Mound to Princes Street. At the bottom a couple were sitting with a large dog, a boy and a girl. Nothing unusual in that. Since he did not have Sophie with him he did not intend to give them anything. He recognised the boy, a sharp-faced lad with a distinctive mark below his left eye, a mark shaped like a kite. He was often there. The girl was wrapped in an old overcoat and scarf while her head was swamped by a moth-eaten fur hat. She wore wire rimmed glasses perched on the end of her nose. Cormac gave her only a cursory glance and passed on. He stopped, looked back. She was looking away, up the steps at a woman coming down and holding out her hand in supplication. It couldn't have been, Cormac told himself, he was having hallucinations. What on earth would his daughter be doing sitting at the bottom of the Playfair Steps begging? He must have been mistaken. And then he remembered that blue and white sports bag with the smelly old clothes in it, clothes suitable for begging.

When he gets in he phones Rachel straightaway. It is her half day at the practice.

'You thought you saw Sophie *begging* at the Mound?' she says, incredulous. 'You couldn't have done. It must have been a girl who looked a bit like her.'

'Remember that smelly old bag I found? Looks like she kept her begging kit in it.'

'But what reason would she have to go begging? She's not homeless or penniless.'

They both fall silent. They know that Sophie would not need to have a reason, not a reasonable one, at any rate.

'She might do it for kicks, I suppose,' Cormac suggests.

'Some kicks!' says her mother.

They discuss what to do about it. Rachel says to leave it to her, she will try to find a suitable moment to raise it.

'She'll probably just deny it,' says Cormac gloomily.

She would have to be caught in the act, as it were. The following afternoon he asks a neighbour who has a child in Davy's class if she would mind bringing both boys home together. He will do the same for her another day. He goes back up to the top of the Mound by the road since, if he were to approach the steps from the foot, she would have a longer run in which to see him coming and make her escape.

When he reaches the top of the steps he sets off running quickly down. He can make out only one figure at the bottom, plus the dog, though there are people in the way, blocking his view, but as he gets closer he sees that the boy is definitely on his own. It is the same one, though, with the mark on his face. Perhaps, seeing him yesterday, Sophie has been scared away. Perhaps he saw a mirage, a false image conjured up by his anxiety for her.

'Spare twenty p. for a hot drink, sir,' the boy calls across to him. There is something about the way he says it that makes Cormac feel that he knows who he is. He stops and rakes in his pocket. He brings out a fifty pence piece.

'Ta. Very kind of you, I'm sure.'

'My daughter, if she were with me, would like me to be generous.'

'Must be a nice girl then.' He is quite cheeky, this boy. He thinks he is being smart.

'You've not got your friend with you today?'

'Got me dog. He's me pal, aren't you, Lenny? Lenny the Lion.' Lenny is comatose.

'But you had a girl with you yesterday, didn't you?'

'Did I? Can't remember. Yesterday's too long ago.' The boy sees another potential customer approaching. 'Spare ten p, miss. Aw, fuck off then!'

Cormac goes as far as the National Gallery, then he turns back. He stops once more at the foot of the steps.

The boy looks up. 'Seems like you can't stay away, don't it?'

Cormac bends over and says quietly, 'Just you stay away from my daughter.'

'You threatening me, then, Guv?'

'Just telling you.'

Cormac walks along Princess Street, stopping at the stance of every homeless person. There's a girl on her own enveloped in a grey blanket in the doorway of Marks and Spencers, and one with a man outside Boots, but neither is Sophie. He goes back up to the top of the Mound and looks down the Playfair Steps. The boy and the dog are gone.

## Chapter Twelve

On Saturday, Cormac, as usual, asks Sophie where she is going and tells her to be home by midnight.

'This time I mean it. Midnight. And not a minute later.' He hopes she senses the new determination in him. He wishes he could put an electronic tag on her ankle so that he could monitor her whereabouts, as he believes they do sometimes with criminals let out on parole. An illiberal thought, no doubt, but he has it.

'I'd better not drop my glass slipper on the way up the steps.' She giggles.

'One of your old rags would be more likely.' Perhaps she is playing out the Cinderella role in reverse. The young man with the yellow-toothed dog seems a suitable candidate for an anti-prince figure. But is he what he seems, Cormac wonders. He, too, might be caught up in a game of pretence. Middle class lad pretending to be homeless? Cormac thinks probably not.

Sophie already has her back to him, on her way out, so that he cannot see if she has reacted.

'Remember,' he warns her, 'the stroke of twelve. Otherwise I shall phone both Tilda and Mandy's parents.'

She turns. 'You can't do that.'

'Can't I? Watch me!'

'You don't know their phone numbers.'

'I got them from your mother.'

She seems about to say something else, then she changes her mind and goes.

The phone rings, and his mother says, 'You've not rung for ages. You're forgetting your old mother, Cormac.' He tells her that she is constantly in his mind and that he will definitely be coming over at Easter, cross his heart he will, and with both children. He has decided to give Sophie no choice in the matter. He has been far too passive. After Belfast he will take them down to Dublin to spend a few days with Sal. He wants the children to know his family, aunts and all; they are part of their heritage, as they are his, whether they like it or not. His mother gives him an update on their activities. Mary. Kathleen. Lily. Sal. Add on his mother Maeve, and you have the five remaining O'Malley sisters. He can visualise a tableau of them.

For once, after her call, he does not feel so depressed. He decides to go out since he is free. The pub is one of the few places a man can go on his own when he is over forty. He supposes he could pick up a woman there but when he looks round he sees as he has done before that everyone is too young. Many of the girls don't even look eighteen. He sights Cathy and Sue, the two girls from school who were on the Paris trip and went with him and Clarinda to the Rodin museum at Meudon. They must have been questioned by the police. They may have given evidence against him. He does not blame them, that would be stupid of him. They were innocent bystanders and could say only what they thought they saw.

*They seemed very close, Mr Aherne and Clarinda*

238

*Bain. They were always walking together, talking together. Half the time they didn't seem to be aware that anyone else was present. She was crazy about him and he didn't seem averse to her either. He gave her a lot of attention.*

It is true: he did give Clarinda a lot, more than any other pupil. And he was flattered by her attention. She was rewarding to teach, to encourage. He was able to put ideas into her head and have the satisfaction of watching them take root and sprout. She listened when he suggested a possible way to lift a piece of work, she'd consider it, and often take his advice, but if she did not she would tell him why not. They had an ongoing dialogue, a conversation that was picked up from day to day. He looked forward to her classes, to seeing her bright eager face as he came in the door knowing she was ripe for development, open to suggestion. So many of his pupils were not. And he did find her attractive, he is no longer afraid to admit that to himself. He found her attractive in every way: physically, artistically, mentally. If she had been ten or fifteen years older they might have been able to form a relationship. There was an undeniable rapport between them.

He orders another pint and leans his elbow on the small bit of bar available. He watches his fellow drinkers as they blow streams of smoke into the air and talk and laugh in the Saturday night crush. They say you can be as alone in a crowd as when you're on your own but tonight he does not feel that. He does not feel a part of the crowd but he is bemused by it.

Cathy and Sue have seen him and are coming in his direction, wriggling their way through the close-packed bodies.

'Hi, Cormac, how are you?'

How are they? he counters. They have left school. Cathy is working for Scottish Widows and Sue is training to be a physiotherapist. And he is training to be a sandwich maker! He makes them laugh. He buys them a drink; they are drinking vodka and coke. They must be eighteen now though they look twenty-five, older than Clarinda looks, for they are well-made up with lots of burgundy-coloured lipstick and eye shadow and sporting trendy Saturday night club wear, or what he presumes to be trendy gear. Clarinda, when he saw her in the library, was wearing little make-up and was dressed as she used to be in a loose colourful dress of Indian cotton.

He enjoys talking to the girls. They chat for ten minutes until they see that their escorts are growing restive and sending signals across the bar. Before they go they say they were sorry Cormac had to leave the school.

'It didn't seem fair to us,' says Sue. 'After all, Clarinda Bain was all out to get you.'

'Boy, wasn't she!' says Cathy. 'She was obsessed.'

He shrugs, says something about water and bridges and getting on with life and the girls say, 'Nice seeing you, Cormac. We must have a drink again sometime.' He says he'd like that.

He leaves shortly afterwards. It is a cold frosty night with an almost full moon, a good Edinburgh winter's night which makes one step briskly out and have the reward of feeling a glow come into one's cheeks. He passes the end of Rachel's street, sees that her car is parked there but not Archie Gibson's. She will not be seeing Archie tonight; she said she was keeping that part of her life separate from the children in the meantime. Davy will be tucked up in bed, content to have his mother close by. They have been discussing swopping the children over so that Rachel would have Davy and he would have Sophie. Originally, they thought a fifteen year-old girl would be better with her mother. But now Rachel is not sure. She clashes a lot with her daughter. 'Could you cope with Sophie?' she asked him. He said he was not sure but he was willing to give it a try.

From half-past eleven onward, he is watching the clock. He is surprised when only minutes later he hears feet coming running up the outside stair. He goes to the door. It is Sophie. She is holding a white tissue to her face but as she comes into the light of the open doorway he sees that blood is seeping through it and running down her fingers.

'What have you been doing?' he cries.

'Nothing,' she mutters, and tries to go past him but he takes hold of her arm. Her cheek has been slashed.

'Christ, what *happened* to you!'

She is crying now and allows him to lead her into the kitchen where he gently takes her hand away from her face. Blood is running down her cheek and down her neck. Angers mounts in him like a raging fire. He wants to kill whoever did this to his beautiful daughter!

'Who did this to you? *Who did it?*'

She shakes her head.

He has to cool himself down in order to help her. He phones Rachel, who comes at once bringing a half-awake Davy in the back of the car.

'We'll have to take her to the Western,' says Rachel at once. 'This needs to be stitched better than I can do it.'

At the mention of stitching Sophie's sobs intensify. Cormac clenches his fists and feels helpless.

'They'll do it as carefully as they can, Sophie love,' her mother tells her. 'They can do it very well these days.' But not so well that Sophie will not carry a scar for life.

They all go in the car to the hospital. Rachel takes Sophie into the treatment room and Cormac sits with Davy in the warm waiting area. Davy dozes and Cormac drinks cup after cup of black coffee from the machine and gets up at intervals to walk up and down in a vain effort to release some of his tension. He feels he could burst a blood vessel in his temple if not his heart.

Rachel returns with Sophie who now has a large white dressing taped to her left cheek. The rest of her face has little more colour than the wodge of dressing. She is slightly unsteady on her feet and her mother is keeping a firm hold of her arm.

'That wasn't too bad,' says Rachel, trying to be bright. 'The scar is fairly near the ear so if she wears her hair long no one will notice it very much.'

Rachel drops Cormac and Davy off on her way home with Sophie. She gets out of the car and takes Cormac aside on the pavement to speak to him.

'Did she tell you who did it?'

Cormac shakes his head. 'No, but I have a bloody good idea. If I see him, and I will, I promise you, I'll carve him up ten times worse.'

Rachel puts a hand on his arm. 'You can't, Cormac. Don't, please. We've got to call the police. We'll do it in the morning. Not now. Sophie is too traumatised.'

The police come to Rachel's flat. Cormac leaves Davy with a friend and joins them. At the sight of the two constables, one male, one female, sitting on the settee, their notebooks in their laps, he feels a lurch somewhere in the region of his stomach but he quells that quickly. They are not interested in him, except as the complainant's father; they don't know him otherwise. Sophie is led unwillingly in by her mother, having vainly protested that she doesn't want to talk to the police. Her parents told her she had no choice.

The woman constable is young and soft-spoken. She sits beside Sophie but not too close; she commiserates, asks her how she's feeling, tells her the scar won't leave as bad a mark as she fears, but they can't let whoever did this get away with it, can they, or he'll just do it to someone else?

'So, Sophie, can you tell us his name?'

They wait.

'Please, dear, you must.'

Eventually, Sophie says, 'Kite.'

'Kite?'

'That's what he was called.'

'He had a noticeable mark below his left eye,' says Cormac. 'Shaped like a kite.'

'Is that why?' The constable looks at Sophie who shrugs.

'Suppose. Nobody ever said.'

The policewoman writes it in her book. 'Where did you meet this Kite?'

'At the bottom of the Playfair Steps. I gave him some money and we got talking.'

'Did you go anywhere with him? Do you know where he lived?'

Again, a shrug.

'Do you?'

'In a squat down at Leith.'

'Do you remember the name of the street?'

Sophie shakes her head.

'If we take you down to Leith could you find it for us?'

Terror shows in Sophie's face. 'I don't want to go there. Please don't make me!'

'Was it there that he cut your face?'

Sophie nods.

'What did he use?'

'A knife.'

'Can you describe it? I'm sorry to have to ask you but I must, you understand.'

'A long thin knife. With a tip. One of his friends held me.' Here Sophie breaks down and Rachel puts her arms round her. There are tears in her eyes too, as there are in Cormac's. His are threatening to overflow, like a dam bursting.

'We have to get him,' says the male constable.

'We do,' says Cormac, who has murder in his heart. If they hadn't called the police he would be out there looking for him himself, no matter what Rachel says.

'Why did he do this, Sophie?' asks the policewoman. Sophie lifts her head. 'He was angry with me. He said I'd set my father on him. He says Dad threatened him.'

Cormac feels he would choke if he tried to speak. Everyone in the room is looking at him. Is it *his* fault? He only wanted to protect his daughter, whom he loves. God, how easy it is to do the wrong thing in this life! 'I told him to stay away from you, that's all,' he says to Sophie.

'It's not your fault, Dad. I know it's not. I'm not blaming you, really I'm not.'

'She's right, Mr Aherne,' says the policeman. 'We know his kind. Any excuse and they get vicious.'

'He had a terrible childhood,' says Sophie, who is still crying.

'No doubt,' says the constable. 'But he can't go round cutting up people, making them pay. Are you sure you don't remember the name of the street in Leith? If we drive you there will you show us? You won't have to go in with us and we'll go in an unmarked car.'

'He'd kill me.'

'Does he know where you live?'

'I never told him. I never let him come anywhere near here.'

'That's something at any rate.'

They take Rachel's car since it will attract less attention than a police vehicle. Cormac drives, with the male constable in the front passenger seat beside him, shorn of his jacket. Sophie sits in the back slumped low between her mother and the policewoman. They drive towards the docks and cross the river and a little way along Sophie indicates they should turn off. They are in a street of tenements.

'There! That one, with no door at the bottom. They're on the top floor. The flat on the right.' They look up but there is nothing to be seen but two blank grubby windows.

They drive back to the Colonies and the police leave them, returning to the street in Leith in their own car, but when they break in the door of the flat they find it abandoned. A pile of human ordure has been left on the floor of the main room; in the kitchen, empty tins and milk bottles sit mouldering beside beer and wine bottles and every kind of rubbish imaginable, so the male constable tells Cormac when he comes back to report to them.

He shakes his head. 'Beats me how a nice girl like your daughter coming from a decent home could have gone there. Unless she's on drugs?'

'She's not. At least I'm pretty sure she's not, not hard drugs anyway. She might have smoked pot.'

'Well, don't worry,' says the policeman before taking off, 'we'll be after him, this Kite creature. We'll get him.'

But Kite is not so easy to be got. He seems to have vanished into the darkness. Now you see him, now you don't. He might have been an illusion, but for the mark on Sophie's face. Cormac keeps an eye open himself. He pounds the pavements, he climbs the Playfair Steps several times a day. Every time he passes someone sitting begging he stops to see if he has a mark like a kite below his left eye.

He'll have moved on, say the police, who are fairly certain he's nowhere around in the city. They have circulated his description to other forces and talked to one or two people who knew him and they say he has gone south. Cormac hopes he's gone to hell. He has always been amazed how people from his homeland who have had close relatives blown to bits by terrorist bombs have managed to say they have forgiven the perpetrators of the crimes. He wonders if his mother with her strong Christian values would be able to forgive Kite if she were to see the raw wound he inflicted on her granddaughter's beautiful face. He decides

246

not to test her. When they go at Easter they will have to think up a story for the wound that will distress her less.

They have other worries. Rachel talks to Sophie who admits that she did have sex with Kite (*How could she, with that young thug?* Cormac is beginning to think he understands less now than he did at twenty.) She swears though that they always used protection. This is something that Rachel herself dinned into her but she takes blood samples from her, anyway. And drugs? Sophie says that she did only ever smoke pot though others in the squat were into harder stuff. 'It could be worse,' says Rachel. 'We are reduced to thinking so,' says Cormac. 'We have been wretched parents.' Rachel will not agree. 'We did our best,' she says. 'You have always liked to take the sins of the world on your back. Please don't take this one on!' She blames this tendency on his Catholic upbringing, he knows, but that is too facile.

Davy goes to stay with Rachel, Sophie comes to live with him. The scar, when the dressing comes off, looks livid. She will never be able to forget the sadistic young man who left his mark on her; every time she looks in the mirror, brushes back her hair, smoothes cream into her skin, she will see it and remember him and the flash of the thin, cruel blade. This is the most cruel thing of all: to be condemned to remembering him. As the scar firms and its edges knit together Cormac sees that the slash was not random; it has the shape of a kite, so even in the heat of the moment - or was he dead cool? - his action was deliberate and executed according to design.

Sophie wakens in the small hours with nightmares and he sits on the edge of the bed and holds her hand until she quietens. He has bad dreams himself during this time in which he is running frenziedly up endless flights of steps, and high above him, always out of reach, going higher as he goes higher, keeping the same distance between them, floats a kite, a black kite. As he surfaces he hears it laughing. He has to leave his bed and go to the window and push it up and stand there for a few minutes breathing in deeply, inhaling lungfuls of the damp night air coming off the river. He smells rotting vegetation. And, in his ear still, he hears the mocking laughter.

Gradually, as the days go by, and then the weeks, the dark dreams lessen for them both. The blood test has proved negative. Sophie stays at home in the evenings unless it is to go to the cinema or theatre with him. But soon she will go out again with her friends, she must. She is nervous about going into the centre of the town though one evening he persuades her to come with him. He will take her to the little French bistro in Fishmonger's Close off the High Street that they have been to before. She clings tightly to his arm as they walk up the hill to Princes Street and then take the path beside the galleries that leads to the Playfair Steps.

'Look,' he says, halting her a few yards from the steps, 'there is no one there.'

There never is in the evening, after dark, especially in mid-winter, with cold skies overhead and the freezing ground beneath. But she is able to walk this way, and although she shivers a little, her step on the stairs is firm. In the restaurant she drinks a couple of glasses of wine and becomes a little tiddly and he is happy to see her laughing again. The young put things behind them more quickly, he thinks. He hopes.

When he opens up the shop in the morning he sees the plain white envelope lying just inside the door. It has been delivered by hand and he knows that hand. He lets his shopping fall at his feet and picks up the envelope. Carefully he slits it open. He takes out a card a of a painting by William Gillies of his garden in the village of Temple under a winter moon. Cormac was always keen that his pupils should know Scottish artists every bit as much as they did international ones.

'I have been accepted by the Slade,' she has written. 'I thought you would like to know. I hope you will be pleased. Thank you for helping me to get there. Clarinda.'

He feels a flush of pleasure. After he has locked up in the afternoon he goes out and buys a card, a vibrant still life by Caddell, one of the Scottish Colourists.

'I am delighted by your news. It is well deserved. Congratulations! With very best wishes, Cormac.' He wishes that he could send her a bouquet of flowers but that might be misinterpreted by Mrs Bain, who has caused sufficient trouble in his life.

His nightmare ended unexpectedly, on a wet and windy afternoon. The weather in the streets was so debilitating that he came home early from his peregrinations round the town. He was wondering what to do with himself when the phone rang and his lawyer said, 'Good news, Cormac old man! The case against you has been dropped. Congratulations.'

He had to ask the lawyer to repeat what he had just said.

'The claimant has dropped the charge.'

'Clarinda has?' He felt stupid.

'Pity she didn't do it before it went this far. Almost to the wire. Put you and your family through hell.'

'What happened exactly?'

'Apparently she walked into the police station one day and told the duty officer that none of it was true. She'd been lying. She could be charged with wasting police time - not to mention everyone else's - but I shouldn't think they'll bother. These young girls! Anyway, Cormac, you're off the hook.'

Off the hook. He felt as if he'd had one in the back of his neck all these months and that he'd been dangling, like a carcass in mid air, feet grazing the ground.

'Thank God,' said Rachel, when she came in and heard the news. She collapsed into a chair. 'What a relief that is! We can return to normal life again. You'll be able to go back to work.'

Archie rang the following morning. 'I'm so pleased for you, Cormac. We all are. As for Miss Bain! I don't know how she's going to show her nose in here again.'

'Oh, well,' was all that Cormac could think to respond.

'Your job's still open, needless to say.'

'It's too late, Archie,' he said. Too much had happened. He'd been to hell and back and much as he had enjoyed his teaching he knew he could no longer walk through that door. And another school, given a choice of applicants for a job, might decide to play safe and go for the other person. After all, there usually has to be some kind of fire to give off even a faint puff of smoke.

'But what will you do?' asked Archie.

'Make sandwiches,' he said as a joke.

He drops the card he has just written to Clarinda in a letter box and continues along Henderson Row to Stockbridge. He could cut down Saxe Coburg to the Colonies but he does not. Part way along Hamilton Place he goes into an alleyway where there is a small colony of studios that are rented out to artists of various kinds for reasonable rents.

When he arrives home he prepares their meal and opens a bottle of wine. He feels he has something to celebrate. He pours himself a glass while he waits and drinks it standing at the window watching the street. He then pours another and turns down the rings on the cooker.

The phone rings. It's Sophie. 'Dad, I'm going to be a bit late. OK? I'm going to eat at Tilda's. See you later,' she says.

'See you later,' he repeats when the phone has gone dead. He sighs.

He finishes the wine of course and eats some of the food, leaving the rest to congeal in the pots. She comes in just before eleven, not too late. Her cheeks are flushed and her hair and clothes look clean. He is thankful for that at least. One has to be thankful for small mercies, he reflects wryly. It was one of his mother's most frequent sayings.

'Sorry about that,' says Sophie, casting a look at the abandoned pots. 'I should have phoned you earlier.'

'That's all right,' he says.

She makes hot chocolate and he accepts a mug though he is not fond of the drink.

'How was your day?' she asks.

'I've put my name down for a studio.'

'Are you going to start sculpting again, Dad? That's brilliant!'

'I'm thinking of it,' he says cautiously.

She smiles. 'What are you going to start with?'

'Not sure.'

'You always said you'd do the aunts one day.'

'The O'Malley sisters.' He smiles now. He can see them ranged in front of him, their eyes fixed on him, expectantly. 'You know,' he says, 'I might just do that.'